"I Asked You To Marry Me,

Logan said.

"I understand that. But why?" Catherine asked. A small flare of hope flickered in her as she waited for his answer.

"Because it would give both of us the things we want out of life."

She knew what she wanted out of life—him. But what did he want?

"Companionship," he continued. "Someone to come home to. Someone to grow old with. Children. We're both healthy, functioning adults, so we shouldn't have any problem becoming lovers." His voice caressed the word. "Should we?"

"No," Catherine said in a small, breathless voice, mesmerized by the look in his eyes. "I guess not."

He reached out, his hand covering both of hers. "You'll think about it, then?"

Catherine sighed. "Yes," she said, because it was the truth. She would think about it. Constantly. Always. Forever. Whether she said yes or not.

Dear Reader:

Welcome! You hold in your hand a Silhouette Desire – your ticket to a whole new world of reading pleasure.

As you might know, we are continuing the *Man of the Month* concept through to May 1991. In the upcoming year look for special men created by some of our most popular authors: Elizabeth Lowell, Annette Broadrick, Diana Palmer, Nancy Martin and Ann Major. We're sure you will find these intrepid males absolutely irresistible!

But Desire is more than the *Man of the Month*. Each and every book is a wonderful love story in which the emotional and sensual go hand-in-hand. A Silhouette Desire can be humorous or serious, but it will always be satisfying.

For more details please write to:

Jane Nicholls
Silhouette Books
PO Box 236
Thornton Road
Croydon
Surrey
CR9 3RU

CANDACE
SPENCER

BETWEEN FRIENDS

Silhouette Desire

Originally Published by Silhouette Books
a division of
Harlequin Enterprises Ltd.

*First published in Great Britain in 1990
by Silhouette Books, Eton House, 18-24 Paradise Road,
Richmond, Surrey TW9 1SR*

© Candace Schuler 1990

Silhouette, Silhouette Desire and Colophon are
Trade Marks of Harlequin Enterprises B.V.

ISBN 0 373 58050 9

22 – 9012

Made and printed in Great Britain

CANDACE SPENCER

was writing computer manuals when she and her husband, Joe, visited New Orleans. Enthralled by the city, Candace returned home and wrote a long detailed letter about her trip to her mother. When her husband read it to make sure she hadn't forgotten anything, he told her she should be writing those romances she was always reading, instead of computer manuals. And so Candace's romance-writing career began....

She and her husband travel often and have lived in a variety of places, including aboard a schooner anchored in Hawaii, the hills overlooking San Francisco, a Greenwich Village loft, the woods of New Hampshire and currently, Minnesota. All of the settings in her books are places she's either lived in or visited. She also writes under her real name, Candace Schuler.

To my sister, Karen,
feminist, free spirit and wonderful mother,
who gleefully filled me in
on all the interesting little facts
about pregnancy and childbirth
the "experts" leave out of their books.
And the two fruits of her labors,
Zachariah and Spencer.

One

―――

Catherine Parrish stared, dumbfounded, across the red-and-white checkered tablecloth at her dinner companion. Her usually serene gray eyes were wide with an emotion very much like shock. Her heart seemed to have stilled in her chest. Her fine pale skin felt drained of all color. Her hand, caught in the act of stirring too much sugar into her espresso, went absolutely still. She only hoped her mouth wasn't hanging open, too.

She'd dreamed of this moment, in one guise or another, for over half of her thirty-three years. She'd constructed misty scenarios of diamond solitaires and impassioned declarations when she was sixteen; fantasized about the what-might-have-beens during the unhappy years of marriage to another man; woven impossibly romantic happily-ever-afters when Fate tragically stepped in and set her free again. And now, when she had finally, absolutely, irrevocably resigned herself to never being more than his good friend, he sat there over Italian rum birthday cake and espresso, looking unbearably handsome and sophisticated, and calmly said the words she'd waited most of her life to hear.

Catherine didn't know whether to hug him or hit him. Typically, she did neither.

"Why?" she said instead, looking down as she lifted the spoon from her cup of espresso. She placed it precisely, with exaggerated care, resting the shallow bowl against the edge of the saucer so its wetness wouldn't mar the checkered tablecloth.

There was an impatient sound from the man across the table. Catherine didn't have to look at him to know he was raking his hand through his hair. "Haven't you been listening to anything I've said, Catherine?"

"Not closely enough, I guess." She lifted the tiny cup to her lips, her eyes still protectively downcast. Her heart, she was happy to note, had resumed beating normally and her voice was as steady as if she were instructing her class of fourteen-year-old math students. Only the paleness of her skin gave away the fact that his words had affected her at all. "Tell me again," she said and took a sip of the strong, sweet coffee to fortify herself. It burned her tongue.

"I asked you to marry me."

"Yes. I understood that part." She lowered the cup, placing it on its saucer. "Why?" she said again and lifted her eyes to his. A small flare of hope flickered in her as she waited for his answer. Had he finally realized he loved her as she'd always loved him? Or did it really only have to do with the nagging sense of "something lacking" he'd been talking about earlier?

Logan Fletcher felt pinned by his companion's steady, questioning gaze. Her eyes had always been Catherine's best feature, he thought. Wide and gray with a thick fringe of lashes, they looked out at the world with a serene self-possession that usually tended to have a calming effect on anyone looking into them. But this wasn't usually. And right now, looking into that cool, expectant gaze made him feel strangely guilty without knowing why.

"Because..." He ran a hand through his thick, black hair again, to little effect; it had been cut to fall back into place no matter what he did to it. "Because I'm forty years old today," he said, explaining as best he could. "Because I've got a ski condo in Mammoth and a sailboat out at the marina, neither of which I've used more than four times, total, in the past year. Because I've got a professionally decorated beachfront apartment, the Jag of my teenage dreams and a partnership in a business I still find interesting after fifteen years. And, as much as it is, it isn't enough, that's why." He felt foolish saying it, like one of those whining, self-indulgent yuppies the media were always writing about. He ran a hand through his hair again. "It's just time I got married, that's all. It's time you got married, too." His intense blue eyes bored into hers as he made the statement, almost as if he were daring her to refute it.

"I've been married," Catherine reminded him. Lord knew why. She didn't like remembering her marriage. And she certainly didn't like Logan remembering it. She preferred to have Logan think of her as ... as what? Sleeping Beauty, perhaps, waiting for his kiss to awaken her? An eternal, undemanding best friend? A—

"For all the wrong reasons," Logan said.

Catherine blinked. "Wrong reasons?" she repeated carefully. She knew she'd married Kyle for the wrong reasons—she'd known it even as she'd said "I do"—but she wasn't aware that Logan knew it, too.

He waved an impatient hand, his Stanford class ring glinting in the candlelight. "Deathless love. Grand passion. All that ..." He hesitated. Catherine was a romantic at heart. Or had been, years ago. She probably still was, although he couldn't think why, with all the grief her husband had given her. "... romantic tripe," he finished, deciding to voice his real feelings. It wasn't as if she hadn't heard them before.

"Oh," she said softly, relieved. "*Those* wrong reasons." He didn't know after all. Oh, she'd married for deathless love, all right. He was dead-on right about that. But it had been for love of Logan, not Kyle.

She'd been twenty-three, quietly dying for the love of a man who couldn't see her as more than his best friend, so she'd married the next best thing. A man who looked like Logan. Almost.

His hair hadn't been quite as thick and black. His eyes hadn't been quite as blue. His chin hadn't been quite as square. His character hadn't been quite as strong. And he had never quite measured up. Not in her eyes and, for different reasons, not in his own.

After three thoroughly miserable years together they'd both been ready to call it quits. But before either one of them had even made an appointment with a lawyer, Kyle had had one too many snorts of nose candy or one too many double vodka martinis or one too many little red pills and ended up just another grisly statistic on a police accident report. Dragged from the mangled metal of his car on a Los Angeles freeway, he'd been D.O.A. at the hospital. Dead at twenty-seven.

Catherine had grieved. Oh, how she had grieved. For Kyle, who'd died so young and so uselessly. For herself, who might have in some way driven him to it, who might have prevented it if she'd tried harder. For all that was lost and could never be regained. But she did it quietly, as she did everything. Holding it all in.

And the world had looked at her—at this quiet woman whose only rash act in her entire life had been a romantic elopement—standing there tight-lipped and deathly pale as her young husband's coffin was lowered into the ground and misunderstood. They had looked at her—*Logan* had looked at her—and seen an inconsolable widow, burying her heart as well as her husband.

It was an impression Catherine had tried to correct when she realized what everyone thought. But since she lived alone, since she rarely dated, since she hadn't remarried and made no secret of the fact that she never intended to, it was an impression that lingered. Try as she might, she couldn't think of a way to let it be known that she'd only married Kyle because he reminded her of Logan—not without just saying it, straight out. And she couldn't do that. It wouldn't have been fair to Kyle's memory and it would have embarrassed her.

So she went on with her life and let the world believe what it wanted to believe. It wouldn't have made any difference if she'd set the record straight, anyway. Logan felt the way he felt, and knowing Catherine loved him *like that* would have eventually taken away the only part of him she could have—his friendship.

"It's been seven years, Catherine," Logan said gently, reaching across the small table. His fingertips brushed back the pale ash brown hair at her temple. He hated to see Catherine sad; hated it with a passion. His palm cupped her cheek for just a moment. "I'm sorry I brought it up."

She shook her head slightly. "You didn't bring it up," she said, wishing she dared to give in to the urge to turn her lips into his hand. But Logan's hand dropped, saving her from making a fool of herself. She smiled with forced brightness, telling herself it was for the best. "It's not that, anyway," she assured him. "I got over Kyle a long, long time ago."

"You're sure?"

"Positive."

"Then there's really no reason that you can't at least consider my proposal, is there?"

"No-o-o," she said slowly. "I guess there isn't. Except..." Her head tilted, causing the soft curve of her classic pageboy to brush against the shoulder of her blue summer dress. "What exactly is your proposal, Logan?"

"Marriage," he reminded her. "I've proposed marriage."

"But what *kind* of marriage?" Did he want a marriage in name only? A real marriage? Or what?

Logan hesitated, trying to find exactly the right words. "Marriage," he said again, knowing no other way to say it. "The kind of marriage that would give both of us the things we want out of life."

"Such as?" She knew what she wanted out of life—him. But what did Logan want?

"Oh, you know..." He shrugged, wondering why she was being so obtuse. Anyone who knew him as well as she did should already know what he meant. "Companionship. Someone to come home to. Someone to grow old with. Children."

"Children?" she said carefully, suddenly very short of breath. A picture of the two of them, together in the same bed, immediately formed in her mind. She could see his body pressed to hers...on top of hers...in hers.

"Yes, children," he said, not noticing her agitation. "That's the main reason, actually. If I'm going to be a father—and I want to be—it had better be soon or I'll be too old to enjoy my kids. You, too, you know. You're not exactly a spring chicken."

"Children?" Catherine said again, very faintly, still enthralled by the images in her head.

"You do still want children, don't you? You always said you did."

"Yes, I do. I always have, but—" She swallowed. Having Logan's children would be heaven on earth but she felt honor bound to point a few things out to him. "Is that any reason to get married to someone you don't—'' she licked her lips nervously ''—don't love?''

''We have something better than that, Catherine,'' he assured her, thinking she was talking about her feelings for him. He knew she didn't love him in the traditional, romantic sense but he didn't want her to; he didn't love her that way, either, and didn't ever want to. ''Something much better.''

''We do?''

He nodded. ''Friendship.''

''And friendship is a basis for marriage?''

''The best. No, listen.'' He held up his hand to keep her from speaking. ''We've been friends for—what? Twenty-five years now?''

''Twenty-six,'' she corrected him.

He nodded with satisfaction. ''Twenty-six years,'' he amended. ''And in all those twenty-six years have we ever had a fight?''

Catherine shook her head.

''A disagreement even?''

''No.'' She was forced to concede. ''But I was a child for a good lot of those years and you're seven years older. That's a pretty wide gap when you're young,'' she reminded him. ''And, besides, as the daughter of your mother's housekeeper, living in your house until I went away to college, well—'' She shrugged. ''I'd hardly fight with you under those circumstances, no matter what our ages.''

Logan waved a dismissive hand. ''Doesn't matter. We got along perfectly. We *get* along perfectly. After all these years, we know each other's tastes and opinions. We know each other's moods, right?''

Catherine nodded reluctantly. She knew his tastes and opinions and moods, certainly. She'd made a career of knowing them. But she seriously doubted if he knew hers as well. If he did, he'd know that she'd loved him almost as long as she'd known him.

"And we both want children before it's too late."

"Yes," she agreed again.

"And it's not as if you haven't already had your grand love affair," he went on relentlessly, despite the pain he feared he might cause her by bringing it up again. But he knew of no other way to get his point across. He was offering her something better, if only she'd realize it. "It made you miserable, if you'll recall. *He* made you miserable," Logan said, his expression hardening as he recalled just how unhappy Catherine had been. "I'd think one experience with that kind of love," he said the word scornfully, "was enough."

"Well, yes." One experience with the kind of relationship she'd shared with Kyle was definitely enough. "But—"

"No buts. It would work, Catherine." He leaned across the table and grasped both her hands in his. The candle flickered in its glass holder, throwing light and shadows across both faces. "I know it would," he said earnestly, squeezing her fingers. "Marry me, Catherine."

Heat sizzled up her arms, almost dizzying her with its intensity, but she forced her hands to remain passive in his. "What about your grand love affair?" she said softly, though it nearly killed her to ask the question.

Logan's brows drew together. "My grand love affair?"

"Have you had it yet?" It hurt her physically, deep down inside, to think of Logan with another woman. She'd schooled herself not to think of it—ever. But now she had to, for both their sakes. "Have you?" she asked again when he didn't answer.

He let go of her hands and sat back in his chair. "I thought you knew me better than that," he said, scowling down at the espresso cup in front of him.

"Oh, Logan, I know you better than you know yourself." She was the one leaning over the table now but she kept her hands carefully clasped together on the tablecloth in front of her. "And I don't care what you say, someday you're going to fall in love with someone and want to—" *Please, God, don't let it happen!* "—want to marry her. And if you're already married to me...well..." She shrugged and tried to smile. "We'd be in a real mess then, wouldn't we?"

He looked up at her, his blue eyes fierce. "It won't happen."

"You can't know that."

"I can," he said with complete conviction. "Or have your forgotten how I feel about that kind of so-called love? Given my..." he hesitated, looking for a way to say what he meant without sounding as if he were blaming his mother, "...upbringing is it any wonder that I think it's an over-rated emotion? A pretty word to make a case of honest lust more acceptable to society," he said, a bitterness he wasn't aware of edging his voice. "Love is a silly, destructive fairy tale made up by people to excuse all kinds of stupid and ir-responsible behavior." His eyes, as they stared into hers, were almost pitying. "I thought you'd have learned that a long time ago," he said.

She'd loved her husband passionately, he knew, though only God alone knew why. The man had brought her noth-ing but trouble and heartache, both before and after his death. Surely she didn't want a repeat of that experience? But what did he know? Maybe she did, he thought sav-agely.

Like a lot of otherwise sane people—his mother most assuredly included—maybe Catherine *liked* teetering on the edge of one roller-coaster emotion after another. Maybe she hadn't married again, not because she didn't want to, but because she was waiting for the man who could make her feel that way again.

Well, he wasn't that man. He didn't even want to be. And if that's what Catherine was holding out for—true love, romantic love, the kind of all-encompassing, destructive emotion that she'd shared with her husband—then he was better off looking elsewhere for the mother of his future children. But, dammit, Catherine would have been so perfect for the kind of life he had in mind!

She would be an exemplary mother. She was patience itself and, being a teacher, she would know just how to instill a love of learning in a child. She would be someone nice for him to come home to, too; she didn't nag, she didn't whine; she didn't throw tantrums; and she never demanded more than he could give.

"Are you sure I can't change your mind?" he said, hating to give up. His long, blunt-tipped fingers toyed with the rim of his espresso cup as he asked the question.

"I wasn't aware that I'd made it up yet," Catherine answered, unwilling to close the door on his proposal quite yet, even though she knew she should. It wasn't the way she'd envisioned it, with champagne and roses and sweet words, but he *had* finally offered his hand, if not his heart.

So... how badly did she want what he was offering?

Enough to take him, knowing she might never have the part of him that really mattered? Enough to live with him and sleep with him and bear his children and never hear the words "I love you"? Enough to ignore the possibility that he might really fall in love someday, despite his protests, and leave her hurting more than she ever had before?

"Catherine?" he said when she'd been quiet for too many minutes.

She looked up at him from under a protective fringe of lashes. "What?"

"Are you at least thinking about it?"

"Yes, I guess I am," she admitted with a sigh, "but . . ."

"But what?"

"Well, we're friends, Logan," she said, staring down at the tablecloth again.

"That's the whole point."

"Practically brother and sister, if you think about it," she went on as if he hadn't spoken. "And . . . Well, I've never thought of you as a lover," she said, managing to voice the colossal lie without stuttering. "And you've probably never thought of me that way, either," she added, getting to what was really bothering her. "Have you?" She looked up at him without quite meeting his eyes, wanting—*needing*—to hear him say he wanted her, at least, even if he didn't love her. "Before now, I mean."

"I never did in the past," he admitted, dashing her hopes that he'd always had a secret lech for her body. "But now, well . . ." He pushed his espresso cup to the side of the table and leaned forward again, staring at her.

She lifted her eyes to meet his squarely. Hopefully. Head-on. "Now?" she prodded.

"You're a lovely woman," Logan said, realizing as he said it that it was true. He'd always thought of her as attractive, with her wide gray eyes and even features. But now he realized she was more than just pleasant-looking.

Her face, framed by the soft bell of her light ash-brown hair, was an almost perfect oval. Her nose was small and straight, her cheekbones high and angled. Her mouth, with it's short upper lip, was lush and inviting and, yet, almost Victorian in its purity. Her chin had the tender, touching roundness of a child's. And her skin . . . Her skin was incredible. Really incredible. As smooth and pale as rich cream, as soft-looking as velvet. He found himself wondering if it was like that all over her body.

"You're a beautiful woman," he amended, his voice low and a little awed by the discovery he'd just made. "A very beautiful, desirable woman."

Catherine stared back at him, wide-eyed with delight, completely unaware of the blush that warmed her cheeks.

"And I'm not exactly a troll," he said, fascinated by the soft color that rose upward from the modest neckline of her pale blue dress. Did it start at her breasts? Lower? "Am I?" he asked, knowing he wasn't.

Speechless, Catherine could only shake her head. *Troll, indeed*, she thought, staring at him. Prince Charming was more like it.

Black-haired and blue-eyed, with the strong features and square chin that denoted character, the rangy, firmly muscled body of a dedicated runner and a smile that he'd inherited directly from his famous, movie-star mother, he was every clear-thinking woman's fantasy. He'd been her fantasy since she was old enough to know boys were different from girls.

"We're both healthy, functioning adults," he added, still staring at her. *Very healthy,* he thought, feeling his body stir to life. *Completely functioning.* "So we shouldn't have any problems becoming lovers." His voice caressed the word. "Should we?"

"No," Catherine said in a small breathless voice, mesmerized by the look in his eyes. He'd never looked at her in quite that way before. As if he were wondering what she would taste like. "I guess not."

"Well, then, there's no problem, is there?" he persisted.

"I guess n—I don't know," she amended, closing her eyes against the look in his. "I don't know."

He reached out, his hand covering both of hers where they lay clasped on the table. "But you'll think about it? Think about what I've said?"

Catherine sighed. "Yes," she said, because it was the truth. She *would* think about it. Constantly. Always. Forever. Whether she said yes or not.

"Good." He squeezed her hands once and let them go. "That's all I ask for now."

Catherine nodded.

"Are you finished?"

"Finished?"

Logan inclined his head toward her half-eaten Italian rum cake.

"Oh, yes, I'm through." She reached down to her lap for her napkin, then hesitated. "If you are?" she said, looking at the remains of his dessert.

"Yes, I'm through, too." He motioned for the check.

Catherine sat quietly, her mind numb, her heart racing, while he totaled and signed the charge slip, completely forgetting she'd been going to treat him tonight in honor of his fortieth birthday.

He took her hand when she rose from the table, tucking it into the crook of his arm as they exited the intimate little Italian restaurant. The starlit night was soft and balmy, the temperature denying it was late January. A warm, ocean-scented breeze tugged at the soft, full skirt of Catherine's midcalf dress, blowing it across Logan's knees as he walked her to her little powder-blue Rabbit.

"Drive carefully," he said, holding the door open for her after she'd unlocked it.

"I always do," she murmured, feeling shy and uncertain. They usually kissed each other in greeting and good-bye. The casual, brief, affectionate kisses of good friends. But that didn't seem quite appropriate now. "Well," she said, turning to get into the car. "Good night, Logan."

He put his hand on her shoulder. "Catherine?"

She turned her head toward him. Quickly. Hopefully. "Yes?"

"Don't I get a good-night kiss?"

Silently, afraid to offer more, wanting to give him everything, she presented her cheek.

"That's not exactly what I had in mind." He put a hand on her other shoulder, turning her to face him more fully, and held her there for a moment, the length of his arms still between them. Giving her plenty of time to protest if she wanted to, he probed her eyes for a sign she was unwilling for him to do what he was going to do. But she simply stared up at him, her beautiful eyes wider than he'd ever seen them, full of an emotion he couldn't quite name. Her body was tense, still and waiting beneath his hands. Her lips were slightly parted.

"Put your arms around my neck," he instructed softly, pulling her carefully, gently, into his embrace.

Silently, her eyes still wide, her body still tense, but quivering now, Catherine obeyed him.

Lightly, chest to breast, their bodies touched.

Catherine gasped softly, then stiffened as a bolt of exquisite feeling shot through her. She'd never been in his arms before—not like this.

"It's just me," Logan murmured reassuringly, entranced and puzzled and excited by the stillness of her, the strange air of expectancy he could feel as surely as he felt the trembling of her slim body against his. How long had it been, he wondered, since she'd allowed any man to hold her like this? How long since she'd been kissed? *What a waste,* he thought and lowered his mouth to hers.

Catherine's eyes closed in sheer, pure, unadulterated ecstasy. The moment she'd waited for, dreamed about, sighed over, and ultimately given up on, was finally, actually happening. *Logan was kissing her!* And not like a childhood buddy. Not like a friend. Not in comfort or in congratulations or in salutation. But like a man who desires the woman in his arms. Like a man who has asked that woman to marry him.

Like a lover.

And she knew, as surely as she knew her name, that no matter how foolish or crazy or doomed to failure it might be, she was going to say yes to his proposal. Because, with just one loverlike kiss, with just one touch of his mouth on hers, she knew she couldn't find it in herself to say no. Not when every cell in her body was screaming at her to say yes.

As it was, it took every scrap of willpower she possessed not to move against him in need, not to tighten her arms in a stranglehold around his neck and beg him to love her always and never let her go. But that was the surest route to losing him, she knew. Logan wanted to marry her precisely because he thought she *didn't* love him, except as a friend. So she stood stiffly instead, holding herself in tight control, channeling all the roiling emotions inside her through her lips.

Tasting her sweetness, her surrender, her brushfire response, Logan felt as if he'd been hit by a two-ton truck. He'd only meant to kiss her lightly this first time, to show her they'd have no problem being lovers. But her lips burned beneath his, driving his temperature immediately higher, making him forget the gentle lesson he'd meant to teach. Who would have thought, he marveled, taking the kiss deeper as his tongue slid between her open lips, that Catherine's calm, self-possessed exterior concealed a creature of such simmering passion?

Her mouth was alive beneath his; soft and inviting; unselfishly giving; full of unrestrained ardor. No, not totally unrestrained, he amended quickly, sensing something even through the sensual haze that was threatening to envelop him. Because, although her mouth was open and avid under his, her body was still stiff and tense in his arms. She wasn't pressing into him like a woman immersed in passion. Her arms weren't clinging to him as he wanted them to. She was holding something back, he realized. She was censoring some part of her response. Inexplicably the thought angered him and for a moment—for just a wild, wanting moment—he considered making her respond completely. Then reason asserted itself.

They were in a restaurant parking lot, after all. And she was right to hold back. It was hardly the place to engage in a full-fledged sexual encounter, especially this first time when they would need time and patience and privacy to get their new relationship off to the right start.

Deliberately Logan pulled back from the emotions she'd aroused in him. Lifting his mouth from hers, he gazed down into Catherine's lambent eyes, his own still fogged with traces of passion. "No problems at all," he whispered with immense satisfaction, already anticipating the time when he could fully explore this unlooked for, unexpectedly passionate side of his serene Catherine.

Two
————

Oh, darlings! That's wonderful news. Simply wonderful!'' Logan's mother, the still beautiful, still dynamic, always dramatic legendary film star Fiona Fletcher, swooped down on Logan and Catherine where they sat on her lilac satin sofa, enveloping them both in a cloud of lilac-scented perfume and the flowing sleeves of her lace-edged, amethyst silk dressing gown. It was four o'clock on a sunny afternoon in Beverly Hills and Fiona was dressed like an Edwardian lady of the manor. "I can't tell you how happy you've made me. How utterly, utterly happy."

She whirled away in a froth of lace before either one of them could answer her, turning to address the more soberly clad woman seated in the lilac-and-powder-blue-striped wing chair on the opposite side of the graceful Georgian coffee table. "Isn't this wonderful news, Irene?" she demanded of Catherine's mother.

"Yes, it's wonderful." There was an expression of quiet pleasure on her face as she looked across the table at her daughter. "I'm very happy for you." Her soft, faded blue eyes touched Logan. "For both of you," she added. "I think you'll do well together."

Logan placed a possessive hand on Catherine's knee. She started, still unaccustomed to these new, casual touches of his, and he patted her absently, as if gentling her. "If she turns out anything like her mother, I know we will," he said, smiling affectionately at the woman he'd always thought of as a second, saner mother.

Irene shook her head at him, an answering smile belying the none-of-your-flattery-now expression on her face. "Well, now." She rose from the wing chair with an air of quiet dignity. "I guess I'd better go and see about some champagne."

"Oh, yes, champagne," Fiona agreed. "Bless you, Irene. You think of everything. News like this definitely deserves champagne." She turned her attention back to the two people on the lilac sofa as Irene left the room. "We must begin making plans right away," she said, her eyes alight with pleased anticipation. Fiona loved a party; the bigger and more elaborate, the better. "So many things to do." She fluttered over to a delicate little Queen Anne desk. "I must start making lists."

"You don't have to do anything, Mother." One hand still on Catherine's knee, Logan leaned forward and plucked a tiny, crustless sandwich off the ornate silver tray on the coffee table in front of him. His mother had adopted the English tradition of afternoon tea about the same time she'd begun seeing the English viscount. Not much of a title, she'd said at the time, but she'd married him, anyway, marking her fourth trip down the aisle. The viscount was long gone, of course—like all seven of Fiona's husbands—but the tradition of afternoon tea had remained.

"Catherine and I are going to have a very simple wedding," he said, eyeing the tiny sandwich between his thumb and finger. "Judge Atherton has agreed to perform the ceremony in his chambers."

"Oh, no!" Fiona put a beautifully manicured hand to her throat, as horrified as if he'd said he was going to be married in a meadow, naked, with a turbaned guru officiating at the ceremony. "You *can't* do that!"

"We can and we are," he said calmly and popped the tiny sandwich into his mouth. Watercress and some sort of herb butter—a sorry excuse for real food. He wondered what else Irene had in the kitchen.

"But I was planning on such a beautiful wedding."

"You can't have been planning very long, Mother," he said dryly, inured to her theatrics by long association with them. "We only just told you."

"I meant in a general way. You know, darling," she cajoled him. "With harp music, and flowers and bridesmaids in lilac satin."

"What if Catherine doesn't like lilac satin?" he said reasonably, as if he actually intended having the kind of wedding Fiona was envisioning—and had had herself, more times than he cared to count. "Not everyone is as crazy about lilac as you are."

Fiona waved his objection aside with an airy flick of her wrist. "That was just an example. Catherine can have pale blue satin if she wants it. Or pink. Or even peach, I suppose," she added musingly. "But not yellow, I think. Yellow isn't right for her coloring."

"Mother, really." Logan was amused in spite of himself. "Catherine and I are hardly a pair of starry-eyed kids. We don't need all that—" he hesitated, searching for an inoffensive word for what he wanted to say "—folderol," he said, in favor of a less socially acceptable adjective.

"Catherine, you can't really agree with this, can you?" Fiona asked, turning to her future daughter-in-law for support.

"Yes, of course, Fiona. I think—"

"Oh, Logan," his mother whispered tragically, immediately seeing she had no ally in the younger woman. It was as obvious as the aristocratic nose on her still-beautiful face that what Logan wanted, Catherine was going to want, too. But Fiona was made of sterner stuff. She hadn't been in front of a camera in over ten years—she didn't like the parts she'd been offered after she reached fifty—but that didn't mean she couldn't still put on a performance when one was called for.

"I want you to be happy, you must know that," she said, meaning it, "and I certainly want you to have the kind of wedding you want," she added, which was a little farther from the truth. "But you must remember that you're my only child and ever since you were a little boy I've always dreamed—" She allowed her voice to catch, just slightly, as if she might cry at any minute. It was very affecting if you'd never seen her do it before but Logan had, countless times, and could dismiss it as the fine acting it was. "I've always dreamed of a wedding here at home," she continued on bravely. "In the gazebo."

She lifted a graceful hand toward the multipaned French doors that overlooked the stone terrace and the gardens beyond. A large, deep purple amethyst in an antique-gold setting glittered on her middle finger. "In June, surrounded by the rosebushes in bloom. Oh, can't you just see it?" she said breathlessly, sounding as excited as if she were planning her own wedding. "With a red carpet coming down across the terrace steps and two little bridesmaids with baskets of rose petals, sprinkling them on the carpet ahead of our bride? And the groom—you, my darling son," she said, her huge blue eyes misting over as she smiled lovingly at him, "in a pearl-gray cutaway and striped trousers. I've always planned—dreamed—'' she amended, "that you'd be married in this house.''

"You bought this house after I graduated from college,'' Logan reminded her dryly, not one whit moved. He wasn't having his wedding turned into a Hollywood circus, like all seven of Fiona's had been. "So you can't have had that touching little dream for very long.''

Fiona made a moue at him, not the least abashed at having been caught embroidering the truth by her son. "Well, if you won't think of my feelings,'' she said pathetically, a mother scorned, "you might at least consider Catherine's. You wouldn't want to deprive her again, would you?''

Logan paused in the act of reaching for another bite-size sandwich. "What do you mean, deprive her *again*?''

"He's not depriving me of any—'' Catherine rushed to say, but neither of them were listening to her.

"It's quite obvious, I should think.'' Fiona lifted a slender shoulder eloquently, as if silently condemning his masculine stupidity about such things. "Catherine had a little hole-in-the-wall wedding the first time,'' she reminded him. "No wedding parties. No wedding gifts. No white dress and veil. No honeymoon trip.'' She sighed and touched the corner of her eye with a delicate fingertip, as if catching a tear. "No beautiful memories to cherish for the rest of her life.''

"That's laying it on a bit thick, Mother,'' Logan said mildly, referring to the threatened tear.

"I got wedding gifts,'' Catherine said at the same time.

"You do know, don't you, Logan,'' Fiona went on as if neither of them had spoken, "that Irene has a beautiful heirloom wedding gown? One that *her* mother wore, I might add.''

Logan looked sideways at his intended bride. "No, I didn't know that.''

"It doesn't mat—" Catherine began, only to be cut off again. But it was all right this time, because she was lying. It did matter. She very much wanted to wear her mother's wedding gown, now that she was marrying the man she loved.

"Yes, and Irene has always hoped she'd be able to see Catherine wear it someday," Fiona went on relentlessly, sensing a weakening on her son's part. "Haven't you, Irene?" she said as Catherine's mother came into the room bearing a large silver tray with the promised champagne in an ice bucket and four fluted glasses.

"Haven't I what?" Irene asked, smiling her thanks at Logan as he stood to take the heavy tray from her.

"Haven't you always wanted to see Catherine in your wedding gown?" Fiona demanded.

"As a matter of fact, I have," Irene said.

Logan looked up, arrested in the act of twisting the wire harness off the top of the champagne bottle. "You have?"

"You never mentioned it before," Catherine said.

"I wasn't asked before."

"There, you see?" Fiona crowed triumphantly. "Now, Logan, really, do you want to disappoint Catherine *and* Irene?" She sniffed delicately. "Not to mention your poor mother, of course."

Logan put the unopened champagne bottle back in the ice bucket and sat down beside his intended bride, angling his knees so he was facing her. "Would you be disappointed, Catherine?"

She looked down at her clasped hands and shook her head. "I could always wear the dress in the judge's chambers." And she could, she told herself. It wouldn't be the same, but she could.

"That's not what I asked." He tipped her chin up with his forefinger so he could look into her eyes. "Do you want a wedding with all the trimmings, Catherine?"

"Well, maybe not *all* the trimmings," she hedged, unable to lie outright while he was staring into her eyes.

"Why didn't you say so before now?"

"Because you didn't ask her, I'll bet," offered Fiona. "You probably just told her what you wanted, just like you've been doing since she was a little girl, and expected her to go along with it, like she always has."

"Didn't I ask you, Catherine?" he said, still holding her chin. "Have I been that careless of your feelings?"

"No, of course not. You're always very thoughtful," Catherine denied. "I wanted—I want," she corrected, "a simple wedding, too."

"With an heirloom wedding dress and bridesmaids and rose petals thrown at your feet," he added, smiling.

Catherine smiled back, feeling suddenly, strangely, cherished. For all his lip service to breathless romance and grand passion, Kyle had never considered her wants if they conflicted with his own. "No rose petals," she said, wrinkling her nose. And then she grinned impishly. "We'd have to wait until at least April for roses."

Logan laughed and leaned forward, kissing the tip of her nose before letting her go. "All right, Mother," he said, giving in. "We'll have the wedding here." He stood and reached for the champagne bottle again. There was a discreet pop as he pushed the cork out with his thumbs. "A *simple* wedding," he reminded her.

They ended up waiting until June, after all, because Catherine wanted to finish out the school year before getting married. Although she didn't say so, she also wanted some time to simply savor the deliciousness of being engaged. She wanted to show off her stunning two-carat solitaire and buy a trousseau and agonize over china patterns and choose just the right wedding invitations.

So they had roses after all. Masses of them. And bridal showers and a catered rehearsal dinner with champagne and silly toasts, and a beautifully simple ceremony in the rose-scented, ribbon-festooned gazebo in Fiona's garden.

The single bridesmaid—a friend of Catherine's from school—wore a tea-length rose crepe with fluttery cap sleeves and a simple headdress of miniature roses and baby's breath. The flower girl was adorably dressed in rose-and-white organdy and carried a beribboned white wicker basket from which she did, indeed, scatter rose petals for the bride to walk on. Fiona was resplendent in what was for her a subdued dress in deep lavender silk with matching heels and a feather-trimmed picture hat. Irene was classic simplicity in a pale blue shantung sheath with a boxy, Chanel-inspired jacket. Logan and his best man were all traditional masculine elegance in their pearl-gray cutaways and white rosebud boutonnieres. And Catherine was radiant in her mother's wedding dress.

Sleek and simple, with long, tight, satin sleeves, a sweetheart neckline that just bared the tops of her shoulders and a smattering of pearl embroidery over the wasp-waisted bodice, it fell in gentle folds to the toes of her white satin shoes. Her hair was arranged in a simple French twist, covered by the heirloom lace veil and crowned with a delicate circlet of pearls and white rosebuds. Her bouquet was a cascade of more roses, blush pink and white, with a white lace frill and white satin streamers meant to drift past her knees as she walked down the aisle.

She wore the traditional blue garter above her left knee. One of Fiona's delicate embroidered handkerchiefs was tucked into her bra for something borrowed. Her wedding dress was the something old. And the delicate pearl-and-diamond drops adorning her ears—a gift from the bridegroom, sent to her room while she was dressing—were her something new.

"You look so beautiful," Irene said when the earrings were fastened in place. The specially purchased pearl studs Catherine had been going to wear were lying on the dressing table, discarded without a second thought. "And so happy." She touched her daughter's glowing face. "I wish your father were alive to see you."

"Oh, yes, I'm happy." Catherine pressed her mother's hand to her cheek for a moment. "Deliriously happy." And she was. Mostly. Today she was marrying the man she loved. "A bit nervous, too," she said, turning toward the bed to lift her bouquet out of its nest of tissue paper. "But I guess that's to be expected," she added, unwilling to admit, even to herself, that her nervousness had anything to do with the fact that the groom didn't love her in quite the same way she loved him. "Weren't you nervous at your wedding, Mom?"

Irene nodded. "A little." She looked down at the fragile flowers, visibly trembling in her daughter's grasp. "But not so much as that."

"I'm doing the right thing, aren't I?" Catherine asked suddenly, like a child seeking reassurance from an all-knowing parent. "Aren't I?"

"You've loved him since you were a little girl," Irene said, as if that were answer enough.

"You knew?" Catherine didn't think anyone had known.

"You're my daughter. How could I not know?"

"He doesn't love me." The hurt pierced through her as she said it, clouding her eyes for just a moment.

"He just doesn't know it yet," Irene said comfortingly, patting her daughter's arm. "Give him time."

"I've given him half my life already."

"Give him a little more," Irene advised. "Be there for him. Give him comfort and warmth and lots of loving. Give him babies. He's an intelligent, caring man. He'll wake up soon enough and realize what a treasure he has."

Catherine smiled crookedly. "That's not a very liberated attitude."

Irene shrugged, unconcerned. "You're not a very liberated woman. Not when it comes to your man." She moved forward as she spoke and adjusted the frontpiece of the lacy veil so that it covered Catherine's face. "Shall we go?"

"Yes." Catherine tucked her hand into the crook of her mother's elbow and took a deep breath. Today she was marrying the man she loved. "Let's go."

Logan stood at the bottom step of the gazebo, the subdued babble of the wedding guests' conversation buzzing in his ears, the snowy white runner beneath his feet blurring in front of his eyes, the stiff white collar of his dress shirt cutting off his air. He ran a hand through his hair, more nervous than he'd ever been in his life.

Was he doing the right thing marrying Catherine? Would she still be his best friend when the ceremony was over? Or would the vows they were about to take change all that?

He didn't want things to change. He didn't want *Catherine* to change. He wanted her as she'd always been: serene and soothing, a friend he could always depend on to take a cool, rational view of things, a woman who shared his opinion that tranquillity was to be greatly desired, a pal.

Could a man marry a pal?

He shuffled where he stood, one finger tugging at his collar, and wondered if he dared call the whole thing off right now. The first notes of the "Wedding March" filled the air. *Too late,* Logan thought. His head jerked up, his hand dropped, his eyes zeroed in on the door through which Catherine would appear.

And then, as he'd been by the first lovers' kiss they'd shared, Logan was nearly floored by the feelings that rushed through him as he watched her start down the aisle on her mother's arm. She was remote and virginal and mysteri-

ous, floating toward him with her slender body completely
cloaked in white and her beautiful face hidden behind the
fragile lace of her veil. Every inch the traditional June bride.
His bride.

He found he liked the sound of that. Liked it a lot. It
aroused something vaguely primitive in him. Something
basic and very male. Despite his nervousness, he was suddenly very glad he'd let himself be talked into this wedding
with all the trimmings. Glad he'd be claiming Catherine in
front of man and God and all the wedding guests. He
wanted this ceremony, he realized, *needed* this public avowal
of their commitment every bit as much as she did. For the
first time in his life, he understood why people celebrated
and sanctified private milestones in public; it made the
whole thing more real than if they merely stood in front of
a judge in some cold, impersonal room.

He held his hand out as she reached him, taking her cool
fingers as her mother let her go. She lifted her face to his for
just a moment and he could see her eyes, wide and shining
through the barrier of the lacy veil. A shy, reassuring smile
curved her lips, filling Logan with a curious peace. Nothing had changed, he realized. She was still the same, familiar Catherine he'd always known, despite her outward
appearance. Together, they turned and walked up the two
steps to the rose-decked altar.

Catherine began to tremble slightly as they listened to the
minister preach about the sanctity of marriage but then, so
did Logan. It seemed appropriate to the solemnity and significance of the occasion. She kept her head lowered as he
said his vows and her hand was icy as he slid his ring onto
her finger next to her simple diamond solitaire engagement
ring. She faltered slightly when it was her turn, bobbling her
bouquet when she handed it to her bridesmaid, but her voice
was calm and clear when she pledged her troth and her

hands, though cold, were steady as she slid the wide gold band onto the third finger of his left hand.

"I now pronounce you husband and wife," the minister intoned. There was an expectant pause as they continued to stand there, staring down at the matching wedding bands on their clasped hands. The minister smiled. "You may kiss your bride," he prompted gently.

Silently they turned toward each other, lifted their heads, looked at each other. Gently, almost reverently, Logan reached out and raised her veil. Her eyes were wide and misted with tears beneath it. He suspected his own were, too. "Mrs. Fletcher, I presume," he said, smiling.

She smiled back, her lips trembling a little. "Mr. Fletcher," she whispered, almost soundlessly.

And then, his hands still holding the edges of the veil, he kissed her.

It was a tender salute, a delicate tasting meant to last for just a second or two, but Catherine felt it clear down to her toes. She leaned forward slightly as his lips started to lift, unconsciously protesting his withdrawal. He paused for a heartbeat's worth of time, as if she'd taken him by surprise. She felt him take a quick, shuddering breath against her lips and then his hands cupped her face, crushing the veil against her cheeks, and he pressed forward again, staking a deeper claim with a demanding stroke of his tongue. Catherine sighed and parted her lips, letting him in.

So incredibly sweet, Logan thought, astounded at the strange dichotomy of their kiss. Her taste was completely familiar but excitingly new, too. She was the same Catherine he'd always known and, yet, not the same.

Was it because she was his wife, now?

"Hey, fella, let someone else kiss the bride," said a voice from behind them.

Reluctantly Logan lifted his head and looked around. His best man and the other senior partner of Fletcher, Bailey and Webb, Ned Bailey, was grinning at him.

"You can take all the time you want later," Ned said jovially, pounding Logan on the back as he shouldered him out of the way. "Give the rest of us a turn."

Logan laughed, releasing his hold on his bride, and Catherine found herself passed around like a new baby at a christening to be kissed and patted and wished good fortune. The famous Hollywood photographer Fiona had hired lined them up for pictures. And then it was time for a champagne supper and cutting the cake and dancing the first dance as husband and wife under the billowing white awning that had been erected over the terrace.

Not a single ritual was neglected, and each was thoroughly enjoyed by both the bride and groom. Blushing, Catherine lifted her dress to her knees so Logan could remove her garter and throw it to the bachelors amid a volley of bad jokes and suggestive wordplay. Breathless and slightly giddy, she ran halfway up the curved stairway in the front hall to throw her bouquet to the excited cluster of women in the foyer below, giggling delightedly when Fiona caught it. Shaky and eager, she changed into her periwinkle blue "going away" suit. Laughing and happy, she grasped Logan's hand and ran with him through a shower of bird seed to the limousine waiting in the driveway.

The white limo, hired by Fiona, was appropriately festooned with white crepe-paper streamers, puffed paper roses in every shade between scarlet and pale pink, and a Just Married sign in the rear window. A uniformed driver closed the door as they arranged themselves on the plush back seat. And then Fiona's face appeared at the open window.

"Your luggage is in the trunk, darlings," she said gaily, slightly tipsy from one too many glasses of California's best champagne. Lavender feathers tilted rakishly over one huge, blue eye.

Logan glanced up at his mother. "Luggage?"

"Don't worry, Irene and I packed everything you'll need." She reached through the window. "Here's the key."

"Key?" Logan said, automatically taking it from her.

"A little extra wedding present," she said, straightening. "Have fun, darlings!" she called, waving at them as the limo pulled away.

Bemused, Logan looked down at the key in his hand. A white silk tassel with a heavy, embossed card attached to it dangled from one end. The key, he read, was intended to open the door of a suite at the landmark Victorian Del Coranado Hotel in San Diego.

Logan hefted the key in his palm, a slow grin spreading over his face, and then dropped it into his coat pocket and patted it into place.

"What is it?" Catherine asked.

He lifted his arm, placing it around the shoulders of his new wife. "A surprise," he said, hugging her lightly. He reached sideways and down with his other hand, grasping the neck of the opened bottle of champagne that sat in an ice bucket at their feet.

"More champagne, sweetheart?"

Catherine laughed and nodded, delighted with the new endearment. She reached for the two fluted glasses that had also been so thoughtfully provided. "Why not?" she said, holding them up for him to fill.

"To surprises," Logan said a moment later, touching the rim of his brimming glass to hers.

"To surprises," Catherine echoed, casting a wondering look at the coat pocket where he'd dropped the key.

Logan settled back against the plush seat, his new wife in the curve of his arm, a glass of champagne in his hand, and a sense of anticipation settling heavily in the region of his lower abdomen.

Three

———

You can put me down now," Catherine whispered to her new husband as he stood in the middle of the sumptuous hotel room, holding her in his arms while the bellman struggled with their mountain of luggage. Fiona and Irene had apparently packed everything they'd need for the weekend and then some, judging by the number of suitcases on the baggage trolley.

"Logan," Catherine repeated when he didn't immediately set her on her feet. "I said you could put me down now."

He'd picked her up as they got out of the elevator, claiming tradition demanded it. "And we've done everything else tradition demanded today," he said, handing her the half-empty champagne bottle he'd liberated from the limousine before he scooped her up.

Catherine had laughed delightedly, wavering between pleasure and embarrassment, and let herself be carried down the hall to their room. Now, however, embarrassment was gaining the upper hand.

Not that being cradled in Logan's arms wasn't a dream come true. It was, but... She glanced at the bellman, standing with his back to them as he hung a garment bag in the closet. He hadn't said a word, but something about the set of his shoulders told her he was amused by them.

"I think tradition's been satisfied, Logan," she said, still whispering. She inclined her head toward the bellman as she spoke.

"Oh, I don't know about that," Logan drawled, making no effort to lower his voice—or her. He'd had just enough champagne to put him in a teasing mood. And he liked the way she felt in his arms, all soft and warm and womanly; it heightened the pleasant tingle of anticipation he'd been enjoying for the past couple of hours. "I kind of like carrying you around like this." He bent his head to nuzzle her ear. "It brings out all kinds of macho instincts I didn't know I had." He growled playfully and nipped her earlobe.

Heat flashed through Catherine's body. She squealed softly, squirming as far away from his teasing lips as she could while still keeping her hold on both his neck and the open champagne bottle. The abrupt movement rubbed her hip against him.

The tingle of anticipation Logan was feeling moved a step closer to urgency. "Do that again," he whispered.

Catherine stilled. "Do what?"

"That." He shifted her in his arms, approximating the movement she'd just made. Her bottom brushed against the fly of his pants. "It feels wonderful."

The heat in Catherine's body intensified tenfold, bringing a faint blush to her cheeks. "Logan!" she admonished, flustered.

"Well, it does," he insisted, playfully loosening his arms as if to lower her again.

Catherine tightened her arm around his neck, arching her back slightly to keep herself from sliding down. "Logan, behave yourself," she whispered in her best enough-of-this-nonsense-now voice. It worked wonders on her class of eighth graders, bringing the most unruly immediately into line. It made Logan chuckle and try to nuzzle her throat.

She clutched the neck of the champagne bottle tighter, holding it to her chest to thwart him, and flashed another quick look at the bellman to see if he'd heard or seen.

If he had, he gave no outward indication of it as he finished with the luggage and crossed the room to draw open the drapes that almost completely concealed two walls of the large corner room. The nubby panels of oyster-colored fabric slid back under his hand, revealing a sweeping view of lighted tennis courts, an olympic-size swimming pool and charming umbrella-dotted decks and terraces leading down to a strip of white sand beach. It was rimmed with scattered palm trees on one side and the placid, moon-kissed Pacific on the other. Violin music and muted, distant laughter floated in with the warm, sea-scented night air as he lifted the window sash. But neither Logan nor Catherine were in any fit state to appreciate the spectacular view the bellman offered.

Her eyes were fixed on the champagne bottle she held clutched to her chest. Her emotions were reeling giddily with the knowledge that she could so easily arouse her new husband. Her mind was groping with the problem of how she was going to keep him from knowing the real depth of her feelings if her brain was going to turn to mush at his lightest caress.

Logan's eyes roved over her averted face, willing her to look up so he could make her blush again by asking her if she was as impatient for the bellman to leave as he was. "Cath-er-ine," he singsonged when her eyes stayed demurely lowered. Why hadn't he realized before, he wondered, how much fun she was to tease? How deliciously beautiful she was when she blushed? "Oh, Cath-er-ine."

She looked up with a quick flutter of her lashes, unable to deny him, or herself. Their eyes met for a fleeting moment, soft gray staring into brilliant blue across a distance of only a few inches. The gray were guarded and flustered and sweetly eager. The blue were alight with teasing good humor and blatant male hunger. Delighted with her, with himself, Logan lowered his left eyelid in an exaggerated wink.

Catherine's blush deepened, as he'd intended it to, and she looked quickly down again, the tip of her pink tongue darting out to wet her bottom lip as she nervously fingered the champagne bottle. Logan swallowed, all desire to tease her abruptly disappearing as he watched her fingers move over the long neck of the green bottle.

The bellman, politely ignoring their inattention, rattled on, making it halfway through his spiel about operating the controls of the air conditioning before Logan gathered enough wits to stop him.

"Don't bother with that," he said abruptly, not caring how he sounded. He withdrew his arm from under Catherine's knees as he spoke, letting her feet slide to the floor. If he held her any longer, he'd drop her on the bed and fall on her like a hungry hound, bellman or no bellman. "We'll figure it out on our own later." He smiled down at his wife, reaching to touch her flushed cheek as if its delicate color fascinated him. "Much later."

Catherine uttered a small, choked sound and moved from the circle of her husband's arms to the window, pretending an absorbed interest in the view.

"Will that be all then, sir?" the bellman asked, not revealing by so much as a twitch of his lips that he was aware of either the woman's embarrassment or the man's growing impatience to be alone with his bride.

"Yes, that will be— No, wait. We'll need some ice for that." Logan indicated the half-empty bottle of champagne Catherine still held. "And we'd like to order up some dinner," he added, thinking to get it out of the way now so there'd be no interruptions later. "Something simple but elegant."

"That's already been taken care of, sir," the bellman informed him, calmly taking possession of the bottle Catherine blindly held out in his general direction. "Miss Fletcher—" he said the name with the hushed reverence of a man who'd seen her earlier movies "—ordered your dinner when she made the room reservation, instructing that it be served within an hour of your arrival," he said, moving to a small round table in front of the windows as he spoke.

Deftly, he rearranged the unopened bottle and two fluted crystal glasses already chilling in the footed silver ice bucket beside the table, pushing the bottle he'd taken from Catherine down into the ice next to them. "If that meets with your approval, sir?" He looked up, pausing as he waited for Logan's nod of agreement. "In the meantime—" he whisked a white linen cover off the table with a little flourish "—there's a selection of fresh fruit in case you want a little something before your dinner arrives." With a flickering gesture of his upturned palm, he presented the table to them.

Small bunches of black and green grapes, plump red strawberries with their stems still attached, toothpick-speared chunks of fresh pineapple and slim wedges of golden papaya rested atop a bed of crushed ice with a bowl of sweet, creamy dip nestled in the middle of the arrangement. A single white rose in a crystal bud vase adorned the fruit tray and, aside from a small pair of silver-handled grape shears, there wasn't a single piece of cutlery in sight. It was the perfect light repast for lovers, with all the juicy, delectable tidbits meant to be nibbled from the fingers. One's own or someone else's.

Trust mother to make sure the stage was properly set for the wedding night as well as the wedding, Logan thought, not sure whether to be annoyed or amused by her obvious machinations. He wondered if she'd arranged for the moon to be full, the Pacific to be calm, and the musicians on the terrace below to be playing violins. He wouldn't put it past her. When it came to romance Fiona never knew when to leave well enough alone.

"I trust it meets with your approval?" the bellman asked anxiously when neither of them said anything.

"It looks lovely," Catherine mumbled, barely glancing away from the window.

"Is that everything?" Logan demanded.

"I believe there's more champagne by the, ah—" the bellman allowed himself a small smile as he gestured toward the opposite side of the large room "—bed."

Logan looked around. Through the wide, open archway to his right he could see a king-size brass bed. Covered with an ivory satin and camel velvet comforter, piled high with decorative pillows, it dominated the roomy alcove created by the short end of the L-shaped hotel room. On one bedside table sat a trio of fat ivory candles in brass candlesticks with sparkling glass hurricane covers. On the other was a Tiffany-style lamp with amber prisms, and a linen-draped ice bucket.

Logan's face relaxed into a rueful grin. For such an accomplished actress, his mother had the subtlety of a sledgehammer. "Well, that should definitely be everything," he said as amusement won out over annoyance. He turned back toward the bellman as he spoke, reaching into his inside coat pocket for a tip.

The bellman forestalled him. "That's been taken care of too, sir." He touched his hand to his forehead in a brief sa-

lute, permitting himself a full-fledged smile. "Congratulations to you both, and enjoy your stay." He let himself out
of the room.

The door clicked shut behind him, leaving the newly-
weds alone for the first time since the minister had pronounced them husband and wife, practically for the first
time since they'd become engaged. They were totally, absolutely alone in a romantic turn-of-the-century hotel room
with the moon shining on the water outside and champagne cooling in silver ice buckets inside and the sound of
violins drifting in on the warm, sea-scented breeze. The big
brass bed behind them seemed to grow bigger as the seconds ticked silently by.

And so the honeymoon has officially begun, Catherine
thought. She swallowed and moved closer to the window,
fingering the drapes as she looked down on the scene below
without really seeing it.

She was as nervous as a virgin bride, as nervous as if she
hadn't dreamed about this night for most of her life, hadn't
consciously planned for it for the past six months, hadn't
already decided exactly how she was going to deal with it.
But maybe that was part of the problem. She'd been
dreaming and planning and this...*this* was reality. Was she
ready to face reality? Could she face it without giving herself away? "It's really a lovely view, isn't it?" she murmured, as if that were the only thing on her mind at the
moment.

She felt Logan's hands close lightly over her shoulders
from behind. "Um-hmm." His lips touched the back of her
head. "But it's lovelier in here." Gently he turned her to face
him, deliberately ignoring the slight stiffness of her body. It
was only nerves, he told himself. And only to be expected
under the circumstances; he was nervous, too. Things were
about to change again. But he was eager for the change this
time. Very eager. He leaned forward to kiss her.

She turned her head slightly at the last second, avoiding his lips.

He drew back. "Catherine?"

"It's nothing, just . . ." She shook her head, as if denying whatever thought she'd had. *Nerves. It's just nerves. You can handle it.* "It's nothing," she said again and lifted her lips to his.

"It's just what?" he prompted, holding her in front of him by the shoulders. He was eager, yes, but he wanted her eager, too. If something was bothering her beyond a simple case of first-night jitters, he wanted to know what it was. "Tell me, Catherine."

"It's just that I . . ." She lifted her shoulders in a little half shrug, like an embarrassed child who didn't quite know how to say what she meant.

"Just what?"

"Well, our dinner will be here soon and I . . ." She looked away, toward the windows, and shrugged again.

Relief flooded through him, all out of proportion to her mumbled words. She was worried about the proprieties again, just as she'd been when he kissed her that first time in the restaurant parking lot. He put his hand under her chin, turning her face to his. "And I'm trying to rush you into bed like some sex-crazed adolescent, with room service about to knock on the door any minute," he teased gently.

"No, it isn't that." But it was. Sort of.

Although she was almost pathetically eager to crawl into that big brass bed with Logan, she wanted to delay the moment, too. And not only because she was afraid of what sloppy, sentimental thing she might say once she was there, but because she wanted all the little steps and rituals that went with being a bride on her wedding night.

She wanted everything she hadn't had with Kyle, everything she hadn't *let* herself have because some part of her— some foolishly yearning, deeply secret part of her—had been saving it in case the impossible ever happened. And now that the impossible had happened, now that she was Logan's wife in name and about to become so in fact, she wanted to draw the experience out, to anticipate and savor every moment—without worrying about interruptions from room service or anyone else.

She wanted to take a warm, scented bath. She wanted to smooth on scented lotion before slipping into the brand-new blush-pink silk negligee and matching lace peignoir she'd searched half of L.A. for. She wanted to brush her hair until it gleamed and to touch the glass stopper of her perfume to all her pulse points. She wanted to primp and prepare and anticipate, all the while imagining Logan waiting impatiently on the other side of the door.

And when she finally opened the door, she wanted to see that look on his face, the hungry, eager one he'd given her in the restaurant when she'd asked him if he'd ever thought of her as a lover, the one she could pretend was the look of a man in love.

But how could she tell him what she wanted without sounding sloppy and sentimental and desperately in love? It would end the honeymoon before it even got started!

"Why don't you go take a bath before our dinner gets here?" Logan said then, belatedly realizing that, aside from worrying about interruptions, she probably wanted to do whatever it was woman did before they went to bed.

Catherine blinked, wondering if he'd read her mind. And how *much* of her mind he'd read. If he knew she wanted a bath, did he know—

"Go on," he urged, giving her a little push to start her on her way. "I'll let you know when room service gets here."

He suppressed the urge to call her back when she turned away from him, tamping down the niggling little voice inside him that wondered if she'd been as concerned with the proprieties on her first wedding night, when she'd been madly in love with her groom.

Room service arrived while she was trying to decide if she should tie her hair back with a satin ribbon that matched her nightgown. She'd read somewhere that some men liked the symbolism of taking a woman's hair down on their first night together. But did the ribbon make her look a bit too schoolmarmish? She tilted her head to get a different angle. Yes, definitely too schoolmarmish, she decided, reaching for the bow over her ear.

"Catherine?" Logan's voice came through the closed door, making her jump. "Dinner's here."

She yanked the ribbon loose and tossed it on the bathroom counter. "I'll be out in a minute," she called, hoping she didn't sound as jerky and unsure as she felt.

She smoothed her hands over her hair and peered at herself in the mirror. The blush pink, bias-cut silk nightgown hugged her slender body in all the right places, making her look more voluptuous than she really was. The matching lace peignoir was as sheer and as airy as a cobweb, edged all around with a deep, self-ruffle that lay softly against her neck and wrists, and billowed around her ankles when she moved. But even without the hair ribbon she still looked too schoolmarmish, too cool, too... ordinary.

She shrugged the peignoir off one shoulder and studied her reflection again. Too obvious, she decided, pulling it back into place. Bending from the waist, she fluffed her hair with her hands, tossing it back with a shake of her head as she straightened. Better? She licked her lips, leaving them moist and shiny. Worse?

"Catherine, dinner's getting cold."

"Coming," she said, still staring at herself in the mirror. Now her hair looked as if she hadn't even combed it. She ran her hands over it again, trying to pat it smooth, her eyes on the mirror to judge the effect. The same old Catherine looked back at her. The woman was dressed in pale pink silk and lace but she was still the same Catherine. Giving it up as a lost cause, she took a deep breath, composed her features into what she hoped was an expression of seductive calm and pulled the door open.

The room was in semidarkness, lit only by the terrace lights shining in from outside, the candles on the table and the softly glowing, amber-shaded glass lamp in the alcove by the bed. Logan stood in three-quarters profile to her, his suit gone, his feet and calves bare, his lean, runner's body covered by the plush fabric of a royal-blue velour robe. The wide sleeves were folded back, exposing his strong wrists and forearms. The lapels were loosely crossed over his torso, exposing the vulnerable hollow at the base of his throat and a deep wedge of his tanned, hairy chest. His head was bent, the candlelight flickering over the angled planes of his face as he poured champagne into the two tall, tapered glasses on the table.

Catherine hovered in the doorway, enthralled by the sheer male beauty of him. *My husband,* she thought, awed. *Logan Fletcher is my husband.* It didn't seem possible. She wavered where she was a moment more, wondering if she should wait for him to notice her or walk across the room and wrap her arms around his waist as everything in her was urging her to do.

He looked up before she could decide, his head turning as if sensing her presence, his hand stilling over the champagne glass. His eyes widened noticeably when he saw her standing there—her slender body sheathed in thin pink silk and filmy lace, her hair full and just a little bit wild, her lips parted and moist. She was the same Catherine he'd always known, and yet excitingly different, too. It was as if a tantalizingly familiar stranger had walked into his bedroom.

Very carefully, he put the champagne bottle down and held out his hands. "Mrs. Fletcher, I presume."

Catherine's breath caught somewhere in her throat; the look in his eyes was everything she'd hoped it would be, everything it had been the night he'd asked her to marry him. "Mr. Fletcher," she said softly, tremulously, stretching out her own hands as she glided across the room to him.

He caught her fingers in his and lifted them—first one, then the other—to his lips. "You're beautiful," he said between kisses. "So very beautiful." He turned her hand over and pressed his lips to her palm. "And desirable." And then her other palm. "And exciting."

Catherine blushed with pleasure. "So are you. Desirable and exciting, I mean," she added when he cocked an eyebrow at her. "And beautiful, too," she said, almost under her breath.

But he heard her. Her soft words had him fighting the urge to pick her up and carry her straight to the big brass bed, to put her beneath him—now! Immediately!—and slake his suddenly raging desire.

It surprised him, that desire. The strength of it. The depth of it. The *neediness* of it. He'd expected to feel desire, to feel tenderness and passion for the woman who'd always been his best friend and was now his wife as well. But the need was a surprise. One he wasn't sure he liked.

"Shall we eat?" he said gruffly, losing her hands so he could pull her chair out for her.

Catherine nodded and sat down, her eyes wide and avid as she watched him walk around the table and seat himself across from her.

He picked up his champagne glass. "To friendship," he said, reminding himself of the reason he'd married her.

Catherine lifted her glass. "To friendship," she echoed as their glasses touched. "And marriage."

Logan nodded and drank deeply, setting his glass aside only when the champagne was half gone. "Looks good," he said, staring at his plate as he picked up his fork.

"Yes," Catherine said, staring at him.

Logan chewed and swallowed two bites of something that could have been shoe leather for all the attention he paid it before realizing Catherine wasn't eating. "Not hungry?"

She dropped her gaze to the table before he could see her eating him with her eyes. "No, not very." It was a terrible waste of food but she couldn't help it; she felt as if even the tiniest bite would stick in her throat.

Logan put his fork down. "Neither am I." He waited until her eyes lifted to meet his across the flickering candlelight. Hot, hungry blue stared into equally hot, hungry gray for a heartbeat's worth of time. "Except for you," he admitted.

"Yes," she said softly, afraid to say more. If she said any more right now it would be *I love you*. And he didn't want to hear that. She stood, pushing her chair away from the table with the backs of her legs. If she couldn't tell him how she felt, she could show him. "Let's go to bed, Logan."

His chair teetered behind him as he came to his feet. He grabbed behind him without looking, righting it, and then swooped around the table like a bird of prey descending on a helpless dove. Without another word being spoken, Catherine found herself scooped up against his chest and carried to the bed. The delicate velvet and satin spread had already been folded back, the decorative pillows piled on the beige satin bench at the foot of the bed.

He must have done it while I was in the bathroom, she thought.

And then the coolness of the sheets touched her back through the lace of her peignoir and the heat of his body pressed against her breasts through the silk of her nightgown and she ceased to think at all. Except of him.

Making love with Logan was both easier and harder than she'd expected it to be. Easier because her soft sighs and murmurs and cries of passion could quite naturally be attributed to sexual excitement. Harder because the three little words she wanted to say most, the three words she knew she couldn't say at all, had to be dammed up inside her. Each time they threatened to break free, she said something else instead.

"Oh," she sighed when he brushed aside the lace ruffle on her peignoir to touch his mouth to her throat.

"Yes," she murmured when he lowered the straps of her nightgown to feast on her breasts.

"Please, oh, please," she cried when he cupped his hand over the moistness between her legs.

Her soft, breathless words and phrases inflamed him, driving his already raging desire higher, enhancing the pleasure he got from touching and tasting her body. He loved how she sighed when he started to undress her, the excited murmurs of assent and approval when he took her hard little nipple into his mouth, the passionate mewling cries when he touched the flowering heat between her slender thighs.

Each barely heard word pushed him to make her utter another, and then another, until all she could do was moan in need. Experimentally, he rotated the heel of his hand against the juncture of her thighs, crooking two fingers to just barely slip them inside her. She arched against him, her hands clutching at his shoulders, the soles of her feet pressing against the mattress, her knees opening wider to invite him in.

"I didn't think you'd be this hot," he said raggedly, resisting her efforts to bring his body over hers. "You're always so cool. So calm. I didn't dream you'd get this hot." He pushed his fingers deeper, pushing her higher, savoring her moans of pleasure.

"Please," she panted. "Oh, please." She was vibrating with emotion, shivering with heat, straining with the conflicting needs to shout out her love and keep it secret at the same time. Almost frantically, she skimmed her hand down his side, over the front of his narrow hip, to grasp the hard male flesh between his legs. "Now, *please*."

His control cracked clean through at her straightforward, passionate demand. With a ragged groan, he lifted himself over her, settling his lean hips between her open thighs, and thrust himself into her body. The cry she gave when he filled her was almost a scream but he knew instinctively that it wasn't one of pain. And even if it had been, he couldn't have drawn away.

She was wrapped around him everywhere—her arms, her legs, her tight, slippery sheath—every sleek, straining muscle clinging so tightly to him that it was all he could do to move enough to complete the act they were both dying for. He could feel her feminine heat pulsing against his groin, feel her heart beating against his chest, feel the soft, excited bursts of her breath against his ear.

"Yes," she panted each time he thrust into her. "Yes, yes, yes, *yes*."

The last "yes" was another near scream, ending in a ragged sob as she stiffened in climax beneath him. She bit down on her bottom lip, her jaw clenching with the effort to hold back the words she wanted so desperately to say as she exploded with glorious, primal feeling. Sobs took the place of words—ragged, panting sobs and murmured, disjointed sounds that could have been anything from approval and praise to pain or distress.

Logan's satisfaction burst from him a moment later, unleashed by the near-wild passion of the usually serene woman shuddering in his arms. It tightened his body from head to toe, twisting deep in his gut, leaving him as limp as a wrung-out dishrag when it was over.

"Catherine," he murmured, when he could speak without panting. Her breath was still soughing against his throat. Her heart was still hammering in time to his. "Good Lord, Catherine, you nearly killed me."

He tried to lift his head to look at her, intending to smooth her hair and kiss her softly, soothing them both with gentle words and touches, but she locked her arms around his neck, silently refusing to let him. He subsided against her without protest, snuggling his face into the curve of her neck instead, and felt her tears trickle down against his cheek.

He knew the intensity of release affected some woman that way, but he hadn't thought Catherine would be one of them. It had probably been a long time for her, though, so maybe he should have expected a stronger than usual reaction. It had certainly been a stronger than usual reaction for him, God knew. He was still vibrating with it.

But when she was still crying a few minutes later, he began to wonder if she'd actually found any release at all. She was still so tense in his arms. Not limp and utterly relaxed as he was—as she *should* be—but clutching him so tightly. He lifted his head against the pressure of her arms.

"Catherine?" He pushed the damp, tumbled hair out of her face so he could see her. Tears leaked out of the corners of her closed eyes, tracking slowly down her temples into her hair. He brushed at them with his thumbs, feeling foolish and inept. A man shouldn't have to ask; it should be apparent from the woman's reaction. "Catherine, sweetheart, did you co—" no, that was too coarse "—did I satisfy you?"

She nodded against the hands cupping her cheeks. "Yes," she said without opening her eyes. Her palms smoothed over his shoulders in small, restless circles. "Yes, of course."

"There's no 'of course' about it." He was just the tiniest bit defensive, thinking he'd been lost in a maelstrom of feeling and she'd been left at the starting gate. And he hadn't even known. "If I didn't, I can—"

"No, no. I'm fine." She sniffed and opened her eyes, belatedly realizing the impression she was creating with her foolish tears. "It was wonderful," she said. "Really," she insisted when he continued to stare down at her. "I was just—" she smiled shyly and sniffed again "—I don't know...overwhelmed, I guess." *With love. With need. With wanting something I can't have.*

"You wouldn't lie to me about a thing like this, would you? I can't remedy the situation if you lie to me."

"No, I wouldn't lie to you. I'm completely, absolutely satisfied." And she was. Physically. A more spiritual part of her was still waiting for completion.

"You're sure?"

"I'm sure," she said, pulling at his neck to bring his head against her breasts. If he kept looking at her that way—so kind, so concerned—she'd start crying again.

He shifted his weight as he came down beside her, pulling her with him so that she lay in the curve of his arm with her head on his shoulder and her hand resting on his breastbone. He lay on his back, one arm securely around her, the other folded under his head, staring at the shadows on the ceiling.

She'd said she was satisfied. "Overwhelmed," she'd said. And all his masculine senses agreed; her body *had* convulsed in an explosive climax. But there was still something not quite right. Something he couldn't quite put his finger on. It was as if she were holding something back or keeping something in reserve but he couldn't think what it would be, or why. Unless—the thought formed uneasily in his mind— unless she was upset because the man who'd brought her to that explosive climax wasn't the right man?

He had no reason to think that, of course. She hadn't cried out her dead husband's name during her climax— "I got over Kyle a long, long time ago,'' she'd said when he asked her to marry him—but, then, she hadn't cried out her new husband's name, either.

Logan told himself it didn't bother him. They didn't have the kind of relationship that demanded passionate declarations and avowals of love in order to make love. They—all right, *he*—didn't even want that kind of relationship.

He and Catherine were friends. Loving friends, true, married friends, but still friends. And friends didn't begrudge each other their memories, even if those memories shut one of them out. It shouldn't bother him in the least that a part of her still belonged to Kyle.

But right then, at that moment, it did. A lot more than he'd ever thought possible.

Four

_____

Catherine settled into her new life with Logan as if she'd been designed for just exactly that and nothing else.

She didn't miss her teaching job in the least; the prospect of children of her own to educate was far more fulfilling. She signed the final sale papers on her little stucco house in urban Los Angeles without a twinge of regret; the satisfaction of creating a warm, comfortable home in the roomy four-bedroom ranch they'd bought in the hills outside the city more than made up for any loss of convenience or location. She traded in the compact that was so good at zipping in and out of L.A. traffic without a quiver of hesitation; the midnight-blue Mercedes station wagon that replaced it suited her new life much better.

It was hokey and unliberated and she would probably be drummed out of any self-respecting women's group for her attitude, but she loved every little thing about being married—now that she was married to Logan. Going to sleep every night with him beside her, waking up every morning with the covers pushed to the foot of the bed by his active sleeping style, finding a stray tennis ball under the couch when she vacuumed, washing out the coffee cup with Marathoners Do It Longer printed on it, answering the telephone call that came, like clockwork, every afternoon to ask if she needed anything before he came home, listening for the sound of his car coming up the driveway so she could meet him at the door at the end of his day—all of it was precious to her.

And nothing she did was taken for granted or dismissed as unimportant by Logan, which made even the most prosaic household activities take on an added luster. Cooking for two was a pleasure for which she was always politely thanked. Keeping house was a source of satisfaction and pride for which her husband was always outspokenly appreciative. Entertaining his business partners and the glamorous clients they managed was a delightful task that earned her a bouquet of flowers or dinner out from the man she'd married.

And, as for the rest of it . . . Being made love to by a considerate, skillful, inventive lover nearly every night was the most exciting thing that'd ever happened to her.

She should have been wildly, deliriously happy. Or, at least, deeply content.

She looked at herself in the mirror over the sink in the yellow-and-white striped bathroom she'd insisted on papering herself. "And whose fault is it you're not?"

But she knew it wasn't anybody's fault. Not really. It wasn't her fault she hadn't known how living with Logan, loving him, day after day, without being able to fully express that love, was going to eat at her. Just as it wasn't his that living intimately with a woman he didn't love the way a man should love his wife, didn't fully content him, either.

Oh, he hadn't said anything—he may not even have realized it himself—but she knew. He was too considerate, too kind, too…conscientious in his dealings with her, like a man who was being careful to thank his hostess for a lovely time. Even in bed.

He always told her how good it was—*and, Oh, God, it was good!*—but she sensed something was missing for him. There was just the vaguest hint of dissatisfaction in his voice, the slightest suggestion of disappointment in his eyes when it was over, even when his climax left him weak and panting and unable to move. She'd tried everything she knew in the past three months, in bed and out, but nothing brought the look of real, total satisfaction to his face she knew should be there.

"Well," she said, staring at the indicator stick in her hand. "Maybe this will."

She was finally pregnant.

The knowledge filled her with a strange mix of feelings. Joy, hope, eagerness, apprehension, resentment. The last was slight but it was there. A baby was what Logan had married her for. Now that he was going to get one, would he still want her the way he did now? Would he still need her? Would he still make love to her with the same single-minded attention? She pushed the thought away guiltily—Logan was too kind to discard her for any reason—and looked down at the indicator stick again.

"I'm pregnant," she said, as if testing the sound of it. She touched her flat stomach with her free hand as if to feel the new life growing there. "I'm pregnant," she said again, staring at the hand on her belly. Her voice was louder this time. More confident. Full of the budding wonder of impending motherhood.

A baby would be someone she could show her love for unreservedly. Someone who would love her the same way; openly, wholly, completely. She patted her stomach, as if soothing her unborn child, and lifted her gaze to meet her reflection in the bathroom mirror. A smile turned up her lips. "You, Mrs. Fletcher," she said, pointing the indicator stick at the grinning, giddy woman in the mirror, "are going to have a baby!"

Logan noticed something different about her when he came home from work that night, something that hadn't been there when he left that morning. She smiled at him just a bit differently when he came into the kitchen through the door that opened into the garage. Her welcoming kiss was just a bit—his mind sifted swiftly through the possibilities—distracted, he decided. Yes, her manner was definitely distracted. Almost secretive, as if she was hiding something.

But what would Catherine have to hide? What kind of secret would—

The answer came to him abruptly, like a swift kick to the gut.

She was pregnant, of course. Wasn't that what traditionally made a woman look the way she did? As if she were lit up from the inside out? Glowing, that was the word. Catherine was quite literally glowing with excitement over the fact that she was finally pregnant.

Not that three months was a long time to wait—the doctor had told them to give it six months before they started to worry and a year, at least, before they did any testing—but Catherine had been worried when she didn't get pregnant right away. He had, too, if it came to that. Children, after all, were the main reason they'd gotten married. Being unable to have children would have made their marriage a farce.

So why did the fact that they were finally starting a family fill him with something that felt a lot like disappointment?

"I thought we'd have dinner in the dining room tonight instead of in the kitchen," Catherine said as she turned away from him to check the pots on the stove. "You have enough time for a quick shower before it's ready if you want."

Even from the back, he thought, *she glows.* She stood there in a pair of gauzy white hostess pajamas with an apron around her slim waist, and little wisps of pale hair curling down from the elegant knot she'd made on top of her head, stirring something that smelled of garlic and ripe tomatoes, and glowed. Stubbornly he pushed away the niggling sense of disappointment he felt at the realization that, in the entire three months of their marriage, he hadn't been able to make her look like that even once.

It shouldn't have surprised him. And it shouldn't have... He ran his hand through his hair. What was the word he wanted? Upset? Yes, he decided, upset was as good a word as any for the unpleasant little feeling in his gut. The fact that he hadn't been able to make her glow like a...a Christmas angel shouldn't have upset him. He'd known going in she didn't love him, that she'd been marrying for companionship and children, just as he had and yet...

And yet, dammit, it *did* upset him! Much more than he wanted to admit, even to himself. Especially to himself.

It made him feel petty and, worse, irrational. Because it *was* irrational to get upset over the fact that he, as a man, hadn't been able to bring the same glow to his wife's face as the prospect of a baby did. It wasn't only irrational, it was— It was injured pride, that's what it was! Just a bit of injured masculine pride, he thought, relieved at being able to slap a label on it.

Logan hated experiencing unnamed, irrational emotions; they made him feel helpless and vaguely anxious, the way he had as a child when listening to the raised voices and slammed doors that invariably accompanied both the beginning and the end of his mother's marriages. He'd learned to ignore the turmoil of Fiona's love life, but he'd never been able to completely conquer the uneasiness that unexpected emotions engendered in him. Being able to label an emotion, to ascribe a logical—if not wholly admirable—motivation to it made him feel a whole lot better.

He slung his suit coat over his shoulder and leaned a hip against the tiled kitchen counter. "Any special reason?" he asked mildly, idly perusing the relish tray Catherine had prepared.

"No." Her back was still turned to him as she readjusted the lid on the pot of whatever she'd been stirring. "I just thought a shower might feel good to you. It's been hot today."

"For the dining room," he said, snagging a carrot stick. It made a satisfying crunch as he bit into it. "Any special reason for eating in the dining room?"

"Oh." She glanced over her shoulder and smiled. "Sort of." She turned back to the counter to pull out the cutting board and began slicing a large round loaf of sourdough French bread.

"Sort of? What does 'sort of' mean?" It was obvious from the coy little smile she'd given him that she planned some sort of surprise to tell him about the baby. He didn't want to spoil it, of course, but it wouldn't hurt to tease her a little before she sprung it on him. "Either there's a special reason or there isn't," he said, reaching out to tweak an errant wisp of hair where it lay against her nape.

Catherine glanced over her shoulder again, her smile even wider and more sweetly secretive. He was going to be so pleased when she told him! More pleased than he'd been over anything else in the past three months. "There is."

"You won the lottery?"

She shook her head without looking at him, busily arranging the sliced bread in a napkin-lined basket.

He gave a pretend sigh. "My mother's getting married again?" he said, only half teasing. Even at sixty, he wouldn't put it past her.

Catherine chuckled at his long-suffering tone. "No."

"Your mother's getting married?"

"No." She sailed past him with the bread basket. "Bring that, would you, please?" she said, nodding at the relish tray.

He followed her as far as the dining-room door. "Too much suspense is bad for the digestion, you know," he warned, enjoying himself now that he'd gotten into the spirit of things. Catherine was always fun to tease; he'd found that out on their wedding night.

She put the bread basket on the table, ignoring him as she stood back to judge the effect, then leaned over and re-aligned it a quarter of an inch. "You've got ten minutes left to take that shower," she said, turning to take the relish tray from him.

He held on to it, waiting until she looked up at him before releasing it. "The contractor lowered the estimate on the pool?"

She chuckled again, unable to keep the happiness inside her from bubbling over. "No." She put one hand in the middle of his chest as if to push him away and then changed her mind, curling her fist around his tie to pull him down instead. She went up on tiptoe as his head descended, and pressed her lips to his.

What started as a light, playful kiss escalated quickly into something else. Something still light but strangely hesitant, strangely rife with unspoken, unexplainable, irrational emotion from both of them—although neither recognized it in the other. Logan lifted his hands to her shoulders, seeking to bring her closer, to take the kiss deeper, to explore and, thus, chart, the emotion he could sense just beneath the surface. Instinctively Catherine leaned closer, opening her mouth under the increasing pressure of his, lifting her arm to—

The relish tray, forgotten in her right hand, intruded between them.

Catherine sank back onto her heels. She loosened her grip on his tie, patting it as if the creases she'd made could be so easily smoothed out. "There, now." The words were shaky and breathless. She'd come so close just then. Too close. A declaration now would spoil everything, upsetting things just when they might finally be starting to go right. "There now," she repeated, forcing a bright smile to her lips as she stepped back. "You go take that shower while I finish getting dinner on the table."

Her eyes as she looked up at him were the same eyes he'd looked into every day since they'd taken their wedding vows. Soft, sweet and shuttered. He dropped his hands from her shoulders, feeling reprieved and disappointed and vaguely angry all at once, and did as she bid him.

He showered and shaved in record time, changing into a pair of casual gray slacks and a dark red knit pullover instead of his more usual afterwork sweats in honor of the occasion. Catherine had taken off her apron and smoothed her hair and was lighting the tall, tapering white candles on either side of an arrangement of pink and blue carnations and baby's breath when he came back into the dining room.

Subtle, Catherine, he thought, smiling when he saw them. Apparently she didn't intend to make him guess very hard. Or possibly even at all. Catherine wasn't one to keep a person in suspense for very long. She was too softhearted.

That's what had gotten her—them—into the situation they were in, he thought. She'd been too softhearted to say no to an old friend when he proposed to her, too softhearted to tell that old friend she still loved her dead husband, too softhearted to say she'd never be able to give herself fully to anyone else.

And he'd been too stupid to realize he'd want her to give herself fully. He wasn't asking for her love, exactly. Not the kind of love she'd given Kyle. He didn't even want that kind of love. He just wanted her to... What? To look at him without the shadow of another man in her eyes, was all. To kiss him without the taste of another man on her lips. To make love to him without the memory of another man in the bed between them. Was that too much to ask?

Oh, he knew she tried to hide it. She was too softhearted not to *try*. Most of the time she was successful. For hours at a time, for whole days even, he'd bask in the tenderness and laughter and care that were so much a part of their life together, so much a part of Catherine, completely able to forget there'd ever been anyone else in her life. And then he'd take her in his arms and she'd turn...not cold—*Lord, not cold by any stretch of the imagination*—but just...away. Distant. As if she were hiding something, or holding something back. Something, he thought, that he just might want for himself, if she'd offer it to him.

Well, maybe the baby was that something. Or would take the place of that something. For both of them. Only time would tell. Until then, all he could do was act as naturally and normally as possible, and try to live up to his end of the bargain they'd made as well as she was living up to hers.

He stole softly up behind her and slipped his arms around her waist. She was still slim and firm, with no discernible changes to her body as far as he could tell. Though he knew she'd begin to change soon, knew changes were inevitable and right, it pleased him that they weren't visible yet. He wanted to be a part of and a party to every single step along the way. After all, that's what he'd married her for. Wasn't it?

"Smells good," he said, ducking his head to drop a quick kiss on the side of her neck.

"Chicken cacciatore." Catherine leaned carefully into his embrace, not melting into him as she wanted to but, rather, just acknowledging she liked the feel of his arms around her.

He nuzzled her neck again. "That, too."

She turned her head a bit to smile at him. "Sit down before it gets cold," she ordered, slipping out of his embrace.

Logan let his arms slide from around her as she moved away from him. "Are you going to tell me what we're celebrating?" he asked as he obediently took his seat.

"Be patient." She poured a bubbling golden liquid into his champagne flute and then her own before taking the chair at right angles to his.

Sparkling cider, he noted as she sat down. *Not champagne.* Another clue, if he needed one. Catherine would normally have served champagne with a special meal; she loved the aura of celebration and gaiety that came with it.

"A toast," she said then, raising her glass. "To you and me and..." She wet her lips nervously. She'd rehearsed this a dozen times since this morning. Two dozen times! And she thought she'd finally thought of something that didn't sound too sloppily sentimental. "To you and me," she began again, "and—"

"And baby makes three," Logan said, grinning at her over his raised glass.

He touched her that night as if she were made of priceless heirloom glass. Each caress was as gentle as a whisper, as tender as a baby's kiss, as searing as a white-hot blade pressed against her heart.

"I won't break, Logan," she whispered as his fingers skimmed lightly—oh, so lightly and gently!—over the flare of her hip to the flat plane of her stomach.

He kissed her just below her navel. "There's a baby in there," he said, awed. "My baby." He kissed her again, a soft butterfly brushing of his lips against her skin, and laid his cheek on her belly. "Our baby."

Catherine sighed and lifted her hand to his head, running her fingers through his hair. She was glad he was happy about the baby and yet . . .

And yet, she wished some of this awed wonder of his, this reverence and, most of all, this new, exquisitely tender emotion that poured from him when he touched her was *for* her. Not for the baby that lay nestled within her. Not for her as the potential mother of that baby. But just for her.

She knew it was like wishing for the moon.

Logan had married her for just exactly this—a baby—and he thought she'd married him for the same reason. He'd be justifiably upset if she changed the rules now. If she said, "Hey, wait a minute. I've decided I want your undying love after all."

Upset, she decided then, smiling a little at the understatement, *wouldn't even begin to cover it.*

He'd more than likely give her one of his icy, disbelieving stares and then run like a rabbit. Or else he'd get very cool and quiet and retreat into himself, which was worse. Much worse.

She'd seen him do it countless times since she and her mother came to keep house for him and his mother after her father died. Fiona would throw a theatrical tantrum at an imagined slight from her director-cum-lover, or dissolve into pretty tears because her leading man—usually both on and off the screen—had forgotten some anniversary or other, or engage in a rousing screaming match with her then-current husband over who-knew-what that usually ended in an equally rousing reconciliation. Fiona thrived on passion and high drama; she seemed to have no idea that her son didn't.

Catherine and her mother had always been Logan's haven at those times. He'd come to their spacious, quiet apartment over the six-car garage—a cool-eyed, tight-lipped teenage boy seeking sanctuary until the emotional storm had passed. Even as a child, Catherine would always do her best to give it to him.

She looked down where he lay with his cheek still pressed against her stomach, at her hand still idly smoothing his hair. Had he, she wondered, been looking for sanctuary when he asked her to marry him?

It was an interesting thought. A pleasant thought. It meant that he needed her. Not just any suitable woman, not just someone who could be a good mother to his children and an undemanding life's companion to him. But *her*. A woman who could soothe and comfort him, who could provide a haven of peace and calm. It meant—maybe—that he'd come to her instinctively when he decided to marry.

What was it her mother had said at the wedding? *"Give him comfort and warmth and lots of loving. Give him babies. He's an intelligent, caring man. He'll wake up soon enough and realize what a treasure he has."*

Well, maybe her mother was right, she thought, smiling. He already needed her; maybe he would wake up one day— Please, God, soon!—and realize he loved her, too. Really loved her, the way a man was supposed to love his wife. The way she loved him.

Her fingers stilled in his hair at the thought, then moved to caress his cheek. She turned his face up to hers. "I won't break, Logan," she said again, still smiling.

He smiled back at her. "Is that a hint?" he asked lazily, rubbing his cheek against her belly as he looked up at her through his lashes.

"Umm-hmm." She tugged on his chin to bring him up her body.

He complied eagerly, sensing something new in her. Something that'd never been there before. He wasn't sure what it was exactly. But whatever it was, she was *here*, eager and smiling, and not off wherever it was she went inside herself like the other times. It would be petty of him, he decided, to quibble because he'd discovered he wanted her all to himself for a while longer—especially when Catherine was so obviously happy about being pregnant.

And besides, he thought as his mouth took hers and his hand covered her breast, *maybe being pregnant has freed her to give what she's been holding back.* Maybe, at last, she would be able to put aside her deathless love for her first husband in favor of the precious little love growing inside her, courtesy of her second. It wasn't exactly what he wanted—he wasn't exactly sure what he wanted—but it was a beginning.

Now all he had to do was turn that beginning into... Into what? What did he want from her that he didn't already have?

Her complete commitment, maybe? No, that was wrong. He knew beyond a doubt she was already completely committed to him; she wouldn't have married him if she hadn't been.

Her complete surrender, then? Yes, that was it, he thought. Her complete, unequivocal, utter surrender to him as a man—as the *only* man in her life and mind and heart.

He lifted his mouth from hers and began a slow journey downward, determined to keep her from retreating behind the invisible barrier she usually erected between them.

Tonight she would be his. Completely.

"Sweet," he murmured, trailing kisses down her throat and the delicate expanse of her upper chest to her breasts. Slowly, and with deliberate precision, he pressed languid, openmouthed baby kisses over every soft full inch of her breasts without once coming into contact with her nipples.

Catherine murmured restlessly and lifted her hands to his head, wordlessly directing his mouth where she wanted it most.

Logan resisted. He was going to take it slowly tonight, very slowly. He was going to draw it out until she was mindless with need. And then he was going to make her say his name before he finally took her.

Bracing himself with an elbow on either side of her body, he cupped her breasts in his palms, pushing them upward and inward so they swelled toward him. His eyes on her face, he brushed his thumbs over her in a flickering caress meant to intensity the ache of desire he could see building in her eyes.

Catherine moaned softly, her lashes fluttering as her eyes closed to savor the feeling—and to hide the love she feared would show through them.

Satisfied with her response, Logan lowered his head and brushed his cheek against the tightly pebbled tip of her breast. First one, then the other, oh so lightly, back and forth, his smoothly shaven skin brushed against the hard little buds in a tender caress. "You're so sweet," he said again.

Catherine arched her back slightly, trying to bring him closer. It felt as if hot little sparks of electricity were igniting between them, growing hotter and more intense with each soft brush of his cheek. Only the firm pressure of his mouth would assuage the sweet ache of desire and keep her from burning to a cinder.

But Logan still held back from giving her what she so obviously wanted, suppressing his own desires until he'd gotten what he needed from her. His tongue darted out, flicking lightly over her nipple. "So incredibly—"

Catherine moaned and arched higher as the heat inside her intensified.

"—deliciously—" He turned his head, his eyes still on her face, and gave the same fleeting attention to the other side.

Her fingers tightened in his hair.

"—sweet," he said, just before his teeth closed, ever so delicately, over her turgid nipple. He tugged on it.

Catherine gasped as a bolt of pure pleasure shot through her. She bit her bottom lip to stop the words she wanted—*needed*—so desperately to say.

"No," Logan said as he felt the invisible wall come down between them. "Dammit, Catherine! No. Not this time." He pushed himself to a kneeling position, his arms going around her waist to bring her up with him so that her bare breasts were pressed against his hairy chest. Her legs were wide open, resting across the tops of his thighs.

Totally surprised by his sudden action, Catherine grabbed at his shoulders to steady herself, then pushed against them in an effort to see his face. What did he mean, *not this time*?

Logan shifted his grip on her, grasping her tighter with one muscled arm and lowered his other hand to her buttocks to lift her higher against him, so that her shoulders were above the level of his. "Not this time," he said again, and bent his head to take her nipple into his mouth.

If he'd been thinking clearly, he'd have been appalled by the desperate sound of his last words. He'd have been aghast at the unspoken pleading inherent in his actions. If he'd been thinking at all, he would have been scared spitless by the feelings that were surging through him.

But he wasn't thinking clearly.

All he knew was that he couldn't let Catherine hide from him again. He had to keep her from retreating behind that wall of hers, had to make her respond completely, with no shadows and no ghosts to temper that response. Maybe he wasn't going slowly now—she wouldn't *let* him go slowly!—but he was more determined than ever to hear her say his name before he made love to her.

He sucked avidly at her breast, his hand kneaded her bottom, and his manhood pressed against the warm female center of her, not seeking entrance, just letting her know how much he wanted her.

Every thought save one fled from Catherine's head. *I love you, I love you, I love you,* echoed through her brain, screaming to get out. She pressed her lips to her husband's forehead, her arms tightening around his neck to hold him even more tightly to her breasts. Without conscious volition, her hips began to move against him in a rhythm as old as the earth itself.

Feeling her response, Logan's mouth gentled and some of his desperation left him. He nuzzled her less frantically, taking soft love bites of both breasts, laving her swollen nipples with long strokes of his tongue. His kneading fingers shifted, sliding down over the fleshy curve of her hip to the unprotected softness between her legs. She was slick with her own moisture, soft and exquisitely hot with a woman's desire. He slipped a finger inside her.

Catherine whimpered, her whole body stiffening as the first shock of ecstasy started to roll over her. "Oh, Lo—" She clamped her lips shut, afraid, as always, that if she said anything at all, even his name, everything would just come pouring out.

Logan withdrew his finger, halting the flow of exquisite sensation. "Say it." He stroked her teasingly, tauntingly, not quite entering her. Once. Twice. A third time. "Say it," he demanded, meaning his name.

"I . . ." Catherine hovered on the edge of frustrated desire and tangled emotions. Did he want to hear her say she loved him? Was he going to say he loved her, too? "Oh, Logan, I—"

"Ah, that's it," he said with satisfaction. "Again."

"W-what?"

"My name. Say my name again."

"Logan," she murmured, still confused. Was that *all* he wanted her to say? His name? Hadn't he heard her say it a thousand times already?

"Again." He slid both hands to her hips as he spoke, lifting her a little away from him.

"Logan," she repeated, deciding that if he wanted to hear her say his name, well, she would say it. As much and as often as he wanted her to. "Lo—"

Her voice caught as he entered her with a slow, smooth thrust.

"Logan!"

"That's it," he said, holding her hips in his hands as he moved against her. "That's—" Ecstasy took him, tightening every muscle in his powerful body. His hands bit into her hips, holding her still "—it," he got out through clenched teeth.

The sight and feel of his release triggered hers. Catherine locked her ankles around his waist and her arms around his neck and held on for dear life. "Loganloganlogan," she chanted mindlessly. The feeling took her completely, threatening to snap the last remnant of her all-too-slender thread of control. *I love you,* hovered on her tongue, clamoring to be said. "Oh, Logan, I—"

"Catherine, that was—" Logan hugged her tight, holding her to him as he lowered her back to the sheet-covered mattress. "Wonderful. No, incredible! You are an incredibly sexy woman," he said, nuzzling her neck. "A sexy, pregnant woman," he added, remembering.

He felt, just then, as if he'd won a major victory—something vastly more significant than another movie star to add to his company's client list, a hundred times more exhilarating than the first-place trophy in a 10K race. She'd called out his name in the throes of her passion in a way that left no shred of doubt that she knew who was making love to her. He hadn't realized just how important it had been to him until it happened.

He smiled down at her, feeling strong and masculine and on top of the world. "You're going to kill me, yet," he murmured teasingly, angling his head to kiss her.

Catherine turned her head away, her teeth clamped tightly together, and willed the tears not to fall. *I won't cry again! I won't.* But it was so hard not to, when she was dying to hear declarations of eternal love and he was complimenting her for an "incredible" sexual experience.

Logan's happy bubble fizzled abruptly. "Catherine?"

"I'm sleepy now, Logan," she said, moving in a way that let him know she wanted him to get off of her. "Pregnant women need their sleep, you know."

She rolled over a moment later, settling herself for sleep with her back to him as if nothing out of the ordinary had occurred between them, leaving him feeling as if... He didn't know *what* he was feeling! But he did know he didn't like it!

Hadn't they just reached some sort of milestone in their relationship? Hadn't they come to some new understanding? And, dammit all, wasn't she going to tell him he had it all over her late husband?

He glanced over at the small mound her shoulder made beneath the covers. Was it shaking, or had he just imagined that slight movement? No, it was definitely shaking. Catherine was crying. She hadn't done that since their wedding night.

But why?

And why now?

And what in hell should he do about it?

What he wanted to do was take her by the shoulders and demand she tell him what was wrong—but he was afraid of what her answer would be. Failing that, he thought about just letting her "stew in her own juices" as her mother would say. He sighed, knowing he would do neither.

She was his wife, pregnant with his child and it was his responsibility as her husband to soothe her when she cried. Words to that effect had definitely been part of his marriage vows, and he took vows—of any kind—very seriously. Besides, to see her cry made him as uneasy as a producer in a roomful of starlets.

Without even thinking of how much he hated messy emotional scenes, he reached over and lightly touched her shoulder through the covers.

She went rigid. He pulled back as if she'd threatened to take a bite out of him. "Catherine?"

"What?" she said in a tight little voice, struggling to hide the deep pain and near panic that lurked just under the surface of that one word. If she turned to him now, if she let him comfort her *now*, when her emotions were so close to the surface, she'd break down completely and just blubber all over him, worse than Fiona ever had when one of her marriages ended. And wouldn't he just love that!

Oh, God, tonight was supposed to be so special and I'm doing everything wrong. Everything!

"Are you all right?" Logan asked, feeling like an ass. *Of course, she wasn't all right! Would she be crying if she were?*

"I'm fine." Her voice was flat and carefully unemotional.

The wall of silence grew thicker by the second as each of them waited for the other to say or do something to break down the barriers they'd managed to build between them. But neither of them said a word nor moved a muscle toward the other.

Five

Catherine stood in front of the mirrored wall between the "his" and "her" closets in the Fletcher bedroom with her arms behind her, tugging at a zipper that was refusing to ascend any farther than the small of her back no matter how hard she yanked. Exasperated, she twisted around so she could see her back in the mirror and tried again.

"Need some help with that?" Logan asked as he came out of the bathroom.

Catherine lifted her head, tossing her hair out of her eyes to look at him as she did so.

He was gorgeous, as usual. His hair was perfectly styled despite the fact he'd probably combed it with his fingers. His bare chest was wide and firm under its pelt of crisp black hair. His stomach was washboard flat beneath the fabric of his black tuxedo slacks.

It was patently unfair, she thought sourly, that he should be as lean and graceful as a panther while she was slowly blowing up like one of those giant Thanksgiving Day Parade balloons.

"I think the darn zipper's stuck," she said, refusing to admit the dress was too tight. It had fit perfectly last month when she bought it for the Baileys' annual Christmas bash. It couldn't be too tight already.

"Here, let me see." Logan brushed her hands out of the way, bending his knees a bit to peer down at the stuck zipper. "It doesn't seem to be caught on anything," he said, grasping the tab.

Except my fat, Catherine thought.

"Breathe in."

Catherine filled her lungs and listened to the zipper teeth rasp against each other as they came together.

"There, that's got it." He started to bend his head, intending to drop a quick kiss on her bare shoulder, then thought better of it. Catherine was a little . . . prickly lately, seeming to prefer not to have him touch her too often, and turning away too quickly when he did. "You just needed a little leverage," he said, turning away to get a white dress shirt from his closet.

Catherine stood where she was, staring at herself in the mirror. The dress was on, yes, but that's about all you could say for it. She could hardly let out the breath she'd taken and her stomach felt uncomfortably compressed, as if she were wearing a tightly laced whalebone corset instead of the light plastic stays that'd been sewn into the dress to support the bodice. The sparkling, silvery blue sequined fabric sheathing her from bust to hips bulged across the swell of her once-flat stomach. The cups of the strapless top overflowed with her suddenly too-generous breasts. Even the multilayered, midcalf chiffon skirt that had seemed so perfect in the department store looked wrong. It hid the most attractive part of her legs while showcasing ankles that were already puffy with water retention.

She'd just been fooling herself, thinking she could still wear a slinky, sexy dress like this! She wasn't in maternity clothes yet, true, but she'd been leaving her jeans unzipped for the past two weeks, holding the open edges together with one of Logan's spare shoestrings threaded through the belt loops. The only tops she could bear to wear lately were the loosest, roomiest ones she owned—or one of Logan's sweatshirts. Anything else was just too tight and uncomfortable, like the dress. But, darn it, she wanted to look perfect for Ned and Barbara's party. It was *important* that she look perfect.

"You look beautiful," Logan said from the closet doorway. He'd been standing there for the past few seconds, watching her survey her reflection. It didn't take a genius to see she wasn't happy with what she saw. "Absolutely beautiful."

And you're lying through your teeth. She didn't say the words but they were there in her eyes when she turned her head to look at him.

The thing was, he meant what he said. She looked absolutely beautiful. Her skin glowed, her eyes sparkled, her hair was thick and glossy, brushing softly against her bare shoulders, her newly heavy breasts were lush and tempting. He even liked the little bulge in her stomach. It added to the earth mother aura she'd acquired in the past month, making her look ripe and maternal and unbelievably sexy.

"I look fat," she said flatly, turning back to the mirror.

"You look pregnant," he countered, smiling at her tone. She sounded and looked like a little girl with her lower lip stuck out. "Just a little bit pregnant and very sexy." He knew she wouldn't believe him but it was true. He came up behind her, hesitating a moment before he put his hands on her bare shoulders. "Very—" he kissed her temple lightly "—sexy."

She shrugged away from him, unable to bear his conscientious courtesy at the moment. She knew very well how she looked. "Nobody's ever 'just a little bit pregnant.' You either are or you aren't."

"And you definitely are," he said, trying to tease her out of her mood.

"I'm not 'definitely' anything," she snapped, unaware she was reversing her earlier statement. "I'm not pregnant enough to look pregnant yet," she added peevishly. "I'm only pregnant enough to look fat." She narrowed her eyes at him. "And it doesn't help when you try to pretend I'm not."

Logan sighed and told himself to be patient.

"And don't get that humoring-the-pregnant-lady look on your face," she began. "I don't need to be—" She broke off, aghast at herself. What was she doing? Logan hated scenes. He hated temperamental women. And that's all she'd been lately. Temperamental and cranky and weepy for no reason at all. But she hadn't gone so far as to actually snap at him before this; she'd been able to restrain herself up to now, no matter how touchy she was feeling. She put her hand over her eyes for a moment, collecting herself. "Ignore me," she said. "It's just my hormones acting up again." She dropped her hand, once again in control of her emotions. "I'm sorry I snapped at you."

"There's no need to apologize, sweetheart." He reached out and brushed the hair at her temple with the backs of his fingers. He wished he dared to take her into his arms but she didn't seem to like being held too much lately. Not since the night he'd forced her to say his name before he made love to her. He was still trying to make up for that. "I understand."

Catherine gritted her teeth at his tone. "I'd better change."

"The dress looks great, Catherine."

She shook her head. "It feels like it's hurting the baby." She put her hand on her stomach. "Like it's squishing him."

"Oh, well, in that case..." Logan didn't know if a too-tight dress could harm a four-month-old fetus but it probably wasn't wise to take any chances. "Turn around and I'll unzip you."

Catherine turned, blinking back tears, and let him unzip her dress. Just mention the baby and he became all concern and solicitude, whereas *she* didn't concern him at all! She expected that, of course, but expecting it didn't make it any easier to bear.

"Catherine?" His voice, full of concern, came from behind her head. His gaze held hers in the mirror. "Are you all right? Would you rather not go to the Baileys' party?"

"No, I'm fine." She caught the loosened bodice to her breasts with one hand and turned to face him. "Really," she said, smiling to prove it. "I've been looking forward to the party."

"We don't have to go if you don't want to. I'll just give Ned a call. He'll understand."

Great! she thought. That was just what she needed—another man who *understood* her. "No, I want to go. It'll give me a chance to meet your new clients."

One new client in particular, she thought. Deirdre Walsh, the newest sex kitten on one of the glitzy nighttime soaps. Apparently smarter than she looked, Miss Walsh had recently hired the celebrity management firm of Fletcher, Bailey and Webb to guide her new career. She'd been taking up a lot of Logan's time lately and, after seeing her show on television one evening, Catherine had been itching to meet her in person. But she'd been planning on wearing a sexy new dress when she did—*not* on looking as if she'd been on a food binge since Thanksgiving.

"Why don't I go call Ned and tell him we can't make it?" Logan suggested again, watching her face for a clue as to her real feelings. As if, he thought derisively, he could read them any better now than he could at any other time. Pregnancy had made her even harder to read.

"No, I want to go. But I have to change first." She turned toward her closet. "You go finish getting dressed and don't worry about me. I have something else I can wear."

The something else was a dress she'd been saving for Christmas Day at Fiona's. Her first maternity dress. Apparently there was no putting it off any longer. Not that she showed, not really, but everything else was just so uncomfortable, especially her party clothes. They all had fitted waists that didn't quite fit anymore, or tops that seemed too low cut now that her breasts had swelled so alarmingly.

So it would have to be the maternity dress.

Cut like a caftan, the floor-length dress was made of silky midnight-blue panne velvet with the sparkle of rhinestones and silver thread on the bodice, and a few artfully random *faux* gems sprinkled down the sleeves like points of starlight. Elegant and quite demure except for the slit up one thigh, it was fashioned to make a pregnant woman feel sexy and sophisticated.

Catherine felt both as she slipped it on over her head. Sexy and sophisticated and blessedly comfortable. She turned slowly in front of the mirror, viewing the caftan, and the silver ballet-style flats she'd purchased to go with it, from every possible angle.

It really was a better choice than the sequined, strapless chiffon and three-inch heels, she decided, her confidence and good humor restored. She looked serenely elegant, quietly sexy and even—she stuck her stomach out as far as it would go—a little pregnant. More than a match for some television sexpot, Catherine thought, feeling quite pleased with herself.

* * *

The feeling of pleasure lasted until she was actually face-to-face with the sexpot. To Catherine's acute dismay, Deirdre Walsh was more drop-dead gorgeous in person than she was on television. Her burnished red hair tumbled halfway down her back and her figure was the kind that would knock a man's socks off even when it wasn't lovingly encased in bias-cut gold silk. To top it off, her wide blue eyes were full of warmth and intelligence, and her smile was as impish and genuine as a favored child's. Catherine immediately felt fat, frumpy and insignificant.

To make matters worse, the casual way Logan introduced his newest client to his wife only convinced her he was trying to cover up his real reaction to the starlet. No man could be that casual and unaffected in the face of such feminine perfection, Catherine thought, not even one who'd spent his boyhood surrounded by beautiful movie stars. That Logan appeared to be unmoved by Deirdre's extraordinary beauty could only mean he was hiding something.

Admiration? she wondered. *Infatuation? Unbridled lust? Or something more serious?*

"Logan tells me you're going to have a baby," Deirdre said when the introductions had been made. "You must be thrilled."

"Yes, I am," Catherine said pleasantly. *Logan tells me you're going to have a baby.* Wasn't it apparent *without* Logan having to have said anything? Was Deirdre Walsh implying she didn't look pregnant yet? That she looked fat? And why was Logan talking to this woman about their private life, anyway?

"I'm afraid a baby's not in the cards for me for a while yet," Deirdre said. "Although, with the way my career's been going since Ned started managing me, and all the wonderful investments Logan's been making with my money—" She sent Logan a wide smile over the glass of champagne in her hand.

Catherine's gaze flitted over to her husband's face to see if he returned it. His lips curved in an answering smile, his blue eyes crinkling at the corners in that special way he had that meant he was really amused.

Oh, God, she thought, *admiration and lust!*

"—I might be able to take some time off and have a baby sooner than I ever expected," Deirdre went on, completely unaware of the subtext being ascribed to her conversation. "As soon as I find a man willing to marry me, that is."

Logan grinned knowingly. "Oh, I don't think you'll have any trouble there, Dee," he said. He knew Deirdre had set her sights on the youngest partner of Fletcher, Bailey and Webb. He also knew Barnaby Webb didn't have a clue that he was about to be romanced by nighttime TV's newest sex symbol. Logan's grin widened. Lord help him when Deirdre finally decided to make her move; the poor sap wouldn't stand a chance.

Dee, Catherine was thinking furiously. *He's known her less than two months and he calls her Dee? He never calls me anything but Catherine!* It seemed unimportant, just then, that everyone had always called her Catherine.

"All in good time," said Deirdre with a husky little laugh and another significant look at Catherine's husband.

All in good time? What does she mean, 'all in good time'? Catherine fumed. *Is that a subtle way of letting me know she intends to move in on my husband?* Pride stiffened her back and brought her chin up. *Over my dead body!*

Catherine slipped her arm through her husband's and curved her spine, sticking her stomach out as far as it would go. The slight mound of her belly barely rounded the velvet of her caftan. *You use the ammunition you've got,* she thought. And being the mother of Logan's son or daughter, no matter how slight the physical evidence, was powerful ammunition, indeed.

"Logan," she said softly, forcing a Madonna-like smile to her lips when he tore his gaze away from Deirdre's face to look at her. "I'd like to sit down for a minute." She managed to sway, just slightly, letting her rounded belly bump against his hip.

Instant concern clouded his features. "Are you all right? Do you need to lie down?" He signaled a passing waiter to take his unfinished drink and wrapped a supporting arm around her waist. "Do you want to leave?"

Take that, Deirdre Walsh! Catherine thought triumphantly. *Now let's see you lure him away.*

She melted into her husband's side, letting him take a bit more of her weight. "We don't have to leave," she assured him. "I just need to sit down for a few minutes. It's so close in here." She waved one hand in front of her face. "I tire so easily these days," she said to Deirdre. It was true enough; she did tire easily. Even if she wasn't tired at the moment. "Our baby, you know," she added complacently, patting her belly. They moved away from the actress with Logan supporting her every step.

"How's this?" Carefully Logan lowered her into the corner of a plump, overstuffed pit sofa. "Comfortable?"

"Yes, it's fine."

"Let me just open this a bit," he said, moving to slide back the glass door that led out onto the terrace. The scent and sound of the Pacific Ocean rolled in with the night air. "Better?"

Catherine took a deep breath. "Perfect," she said. It really *had* been close in the room, so she wasn't a complete faker.

Logan crouched beside the sofa. "Here, let's get your feet up." He put his hand under her ankles, slipped her shoes off and lifted her feet to the sofa almost before she knew what he intended.

"That's not necessary, Logan, really," she said, trying to swing her feet back to the floor. "I feel fine. Now," she tacked on hastily, in case he questioned her quick recovery.

Logan pressed her back into the corner of the sofa. "There's no need to take any chances. You just stay here and rest while I find you some—" *What were pregnant women allowed to drink?* "—orange juice," he decided. "Okay?"

"I feel like a fool," Catherine muttered. Drawing her husband's attention away from a scheming starlet was one thing, drawing the attention of an entire roomful of her husband's business associates was another thing entirely. She felt as if everyone was staring at her.

"It's not foolish to put your feet up when you're pregnant. Tell her it's not foolish, Barbara," he said to their hostess as she hurried over to see what was wrong.

"Of course it's not," Barbara Bailey said soothingly. "What would be foolish is to take any unnecessary chances when you're pregnant."

"See?" Logan said.

"Why don't you go rescue Ned?" Barbara suggested, tilting her head toward her husband. "He's been trapped over there by that game show person for the past twenty minutes. I'm sure he'd appreciate your interference." The stiff green taffeta of her full skirt rustled pleasantly as she sat down beside Catherine. "I'll look after your wife."

"I'm *fine*," Catherine said when he hesitated. "Really."

"Men," Barbara said fondly, smiling at his back as he made his way across the room to her husband. "Even the most levelheaded of them tend to get a little weird when faced with imminent fatherhood." She turned her smile on Catherine. "Ned used to set an alarm so I'd be sure to take my vitamins precisely on time when I was pregnant," she said. "He was afraid something awful would happen if I didn't take them at the same time every day."

Catherine smiled back. "Logan's not that bad. At least—"

"—not yet," they both said at the same time.

"Well, now," Barbara said briskly when their mutual laughter at the strange little quirks of expectant fathers had subsided. "How are you really feeling? Any unusual pain anywhere?" Barbara had been a nurse before she married Ned.

Catherine grimaced comically. "Define unusual."

"Believe me, you'll know if any of the strange little pangs and pains you're feeling are unusual."

"Nothing unusual, then," Catherine said. "I was just feeling a little tired and Logan overreacted." *Because I suggested there was more to it than simple fatigue.*

Barbara patted her hand. "Better than underreacting, I always say." She stood, ready to return to her hostessing duties. "Can I get you anything? Something to drink?"

"Logan's getting me an orange juice. I'm sure he'll be back in a minute."

But it took Logan almost thirty minutes to return with her orange juice, and it wasn't until Barbara reminded him that he remembered it.

Catherine watched him from where she reclined in the corner of the sofa, wavering between wifely pride at his popularity and feminine pique at the lapse in his attention to her needs. He was so sophisticated and urbane in his formal black-and-white evening clothes, so charming with his easy smile and sparkling blue eyes, so ruggedly masculine with his blunt square chin and his wide shoulders. And so obviously not in love with his wife as he prowled through the crush of merrymakers, smiling at all and sundry.

He presented an almost irresistible temptation for any woman on the make. And there were plenty of them at Ned and Barbara's party. Gorgeous women. Talented women. Intelligent women.

And Deirdre Walsh, who was all that and more.

And here I am, stuck in a corner of the sofa like a dis-carded baby machine! That it was her own fault didn't help much. That Logan never actually exchanged another word with the beautiful redhead didn't help much, either.

They did exchange a couple of smiles in passing, a few secret looks and, once, when Deirdre dragged Barnaby Webb onto the tiny makeshift dance floor in front of the ten-foot Christmas tree, Logan grinned and wagged his index finger at her as if she were being a naughty girl. Deirdre merely laughed that low, sultry laugh of hers—Catherine couldn't hear it from where she sat but she knew how it sounded—and snuggled a little closer to Barnaby. Logan watched them dance for a moment longer, his grin never faltering.

Because he knows full well, Catherine thought, that stodgy, well-bred Barnaby Webb, no matter how good-looking in his own way, was no match for the masculine splendor of Logan Fletcher.

No man was, she thought sadly, staring down at her hands. They were folded protectively over the slight swell of her belly. *At least I've got you,* she thought. She sighed and looked up just as a frosty glass of orange juice appeared in front of her nose.

"Here you are. Fresh o.j.," Logan said. "Maria squeezed it." Maria was the Baileys' maid. "Said it had more vitamins than the frozen kind."

Catherine took it with a murmured, "Thank you."

"I'm sorry I took so long." He pushed aside the skirt of her velvet caftan and sat down. "Ned had someone he wanted me to talk to and, well—" he shrugged his broad shoulders, drawing the eye of nearly every woman in the room "—you know how it is."

"Yes," Catherine murmured. "I know how it is."

Logan's blue eyes narrowed at her subdued tone. Catherine was a quiet, soft-spoken woman, true, but *this* soft-spoken? She sounded as if she'd lost her last friend in the world! Maybe she was feeling worse than she let on. Lord knew, she was entitled. He'd read enough about pregnancy in the past four months—especially first-time pregnancies in women over thirty—to have a healthy respect for all her body was going through. Whether it showed much or not, she was undergoing some really awesome changes. Physically and psychologically.

Just reading about it was enough to exhaust him; he could hardly blame her for getting moody and morose once in a while. He just wished she'd share some of what she was feeling with him instead of bottling it all up inside her. After all, it was his baby, too.

He wanted to tell her just to let it all out. *Yell at me if you want to,* he thought. *Tell me I'm an insensitive clod. Blame me for your weight gain and your moodiness and your fatigue. I can take it.*

He *wanted* to take it, wanted to help, wanted to know, dammit, what she was feeling!

He'd tried asking her, once or twice. Did her back hurt? Were her breasts too tender to touch? Would she like him to rub her feet? Did she want a pillow or a drink of water or a pickle? But she always put him off. "I feel fine," she'd say. "Don't worry about me," she'd say. "It's nothing. Just ignore me when I act a little crazy," she'd say as she eased out of his arms.

He knew Catherine wasn't a complainer, of course. She didn't whine or nag or demand extra attention. But, dammit, she was entitled to a little extra attention now. And he was entitled to give it to her. Hell, he wanted to *lavish* her with attention.

Still, he was an adult. He could accept that she didn't want to be fussed over but—and it made him feel like a selfish pig even to think about it—she'd been withdrawing more and more from him physically, too, turning away from even the most casual embrace.

He knew it was partly his fault because of that stupid, macho stunt he'd pulled on the night she'd told him she was pregnant. He'd tried to make up for it, tried to be as undemanding a lover as possible. The trouble was, the more pregnant she got, the less of a lover she wanted him to be.

Oh, he'd read about how some women lost all desire for physical contact when they were pregnant, but all desire to be touched at all? To be held and comforted by the father of her baby?

He wished he dared to just *ask* her what the real problem was but he was still afraid of what her answer would be. She might tell him she hadn't gotten over her first husband, after all, and she'd given up trying. Or even worse, that she wished the baby she was carrying was Kyle's and not his. Just the thought made him ache, somewhere deep inside him. He didn't know *why* it should be so, only that it was.

He reached out to touch her, needing the feel of her soft flesh to drive the ache away. He didn't know why that should be so, either, nor did he think to question it just then.

"I think we've done our duty to the partnership," he said, resisting the urge to run his fingers through the soft hair at her temple. "Feel like heading for home?"

Six

Everything fell into place for Logan when they got home. He pulled into the garage and set the parking brake, turning to his dozing wife to let her know they were there, and it just . . . fell into place. Without the fanfare or melodrama that usually accompanied such revelations, without even a single comforting shred of doubt, he knew.

He was in love with her.

She wasn't just a suitable wife and excellent mother material. She wasn't just his best friend. She was the woman he loved. Desperately.

That's what that damnable ache in his gut was. Love. He should have known! What else in the world could make an otherwise sane, reasonable man feel all the crazy, unreasonable, heretofore unexplainable emotions he'd been feeling lately?

Love was the reason he'd felt that vague, disturbing disappointment instead of unalloyed joy when she'd gotten pregnant so quickly; like any lovesick idiot, he'd wanted her to himself for a while longer. Love was the reason he'd needed to hear his name when she was in his arms. Love was the reason he was so pathetically eager to erase her slightest frown and indulge her slightest whim, even when she insisted she wasn't frowning and didn't have any pregnant lady whims. And love, dammit, was the reason the need to touch her was sometimes so strong his insides ached.

Hadn't he watched his mother suffer—no, *celebrate!*—the same symptoms more times than he could count? Hadn't he watched the men who were in love with her turn into babbling, moonstruck idiots? And now the impossible had happened. He'd joined the ranks. He, Logan Fletcher, was as much of a babbling idiot as any one of Fiona's lovers had ever been.

What else could it be *but* love?

Maybe lust, he thought hopefully.

He considered that for a moment. Lust was the logical explanation, the reasonable explanation, the *only* explanation he would have accepted until just this minute. It was what he'd always believed made otherwise normal people act as if they had no sense at all, what he'd always felt people really meant when they spoke of love.

Yes, what he was feeling could definitely be lust. After all, he hadn't felt this ache when they were having sizzling sex almost every night, had he? No, it had only been since she'd begun drawing away from him physically that he'd—

No, that was a lie. He'd felt the ache before, and worse, when she responded to him physically while shutting him out emotionally. It wasn't her body he wanted, not exclusively, anyway, it was her love—that elusive something she held back, that tantalizing, tormenting something that kept her separate from him even when she was convulsed with ecstasy in his arms, that suddenly much-to-be-desired emotion that, up to this very moment, he hadn't believed really existed.

What a stupid, miserable situation! If it didn't make him so damn mad, he'd laugh. *Him, of all people, to fall in love!* He knew, so well, what a sticky, unsettling mess it made of life. Especially when only one person felt it.

So what was he going to do about it?

His first thought was to simply ignore it and hope it died a natural death before it caused any lasting damage, but he feared it was already too late for that. His second impulse was to run as far and as fast as he could, but that was out of the question, too. He'd married her and she was carrying his child. Besides, he didn't really want to do either of those things, anyway. No, what he *really* wanted to do was make her—somehow, someway—fall in love with him. Surely, he thought, it should be possible.

After all, he'd fallen in love with her—practically against his will and without even realizing it—so it should be fairly easy to make Catherine, who already believed in love, fall into it with him.

She cared about him, didn't she? She respected him enough to have agreed to marry him and bear his children. She responded to him in bed—most of the time, anyway. And they were, as he'd said when he proposed, the very best of friends. They'd both considered that relationship enough of a basis for marriage and parenthood. Surely it was enough of a basis for love?

The question was, how did a man go about making a woman fall in love with him? Especially when he'd already done all the usual things without even knowing he was doing them, and they hadn't worked? He'd showered her with all the material advantages at his disposal, he'd made love to her with all the skill and tenderness at his command, he'd been as understanding and considerate as he knew how to be. Any reasonable woman, he thought irritably, would be wildly in love with him by now!

But, then, he reminded himself, a woman in love isn't reasonable. And Catherine was a woman in love—with the memory of her dead husband.

So he was right back where he started. Crazily, unreasonably, irrationally in love with a woman who didn't love him, without a clue as to what to do about it.

It filled him with a crazy kind of joy.

It made him mad as hell.

It scared him spitless.

He wanted to take her by the shoulders and shake her until her teeth rattled for making it happen. He also wanted to take her in his arms and make hot, sweet love to her until the memory of her first husband was burned away and all she could think of was *him*. But he'd already tried that, and what had it gotten him? He reached out, not knowing which course he would take, and touched her shoulder.

She was sleeping so deeply she didn't even stir. Her cheeks were flushed, her lips moist and slightly parted, like an exhausted child who'd finally succumbed after a hard day's play. Her fingers were laced over the soft swell of her stomach, silent testimony to the reason for her exhaustion. She looked as vulnerable and defenseless as the new life cradled beneath her hands.

Tenderness flooded through him, swamping all the other emotions that had momentarily gripped him.

She wasn't responsible for his feelings and it wasn't fair to take his frustration out on her. It also wasn't fair to make her aware of those feelings when she didn't return them. Especially not now, when the distress and guilt of knowing he loved her when she didn't love him would only add to the stress of her pregnancy. Not that she should feel any guilt over what wasn't her fault but, knowing Catherine, she would. She'd fret and worry and be completely unable to relax and act naturally around him, afraid any little thing she did—or didn't do—would cause him pain. To be always on edge wouldn't be good for her or the baby. He sighed, knowing what he felt for her would have to stay hidden, at least until after their son or daughter was born.

"Catherine?" He shook her shoulder gently. "Catherine, sweetheart, we're home."

She turned toward him with a little snuggling motion, her head tilting so that her cheek brushed the back of his hand, but didn't wake.

So sweet, he thought. *So trusting. So naturally loving.* It shouldn't be hard, after the baby was born, to get her to direct some of that love his way.

He got out of the car and, after opening the door to the kitchen, came around to her side. Bending, he unfastened her seat belt, then lifted her into his arms.

She murmured restlessly.

"Shhh," he soothed. "It's just me."

"Logan?" The word was a soft breath of air against his neck as her head rolled against his shoulder. She yawned. "So sleepy."

"Go back to sleep, then," he advised, smiling when she looped her arms around his neck and snuggled into his embrace as trustingly as a kitten in familiar hands.

No, he thought then, as he moved quietly through the dark, silent house with his sleeping wife in his arms, *it shouldn't be difficult at all to make Catherine fall in love.*

She had so much love to give and she was, he thought hopefully, already half in love with him. With care and consideration before the baby was born, and scrupulous attention to all the little details of romance women found so important, after she'd given birth, he could win her completely. Until then he wouldn't press her in any way. Not emotionally, not physically, not in any way at all. He'd give her only just as much loving attention as she seemed willing to accept until, finally, she'd be willing to accept everything he had to give.

What would happen after that, when her love had been unleashed and directed toward him, he didn't know. Catherine was a serene, soft-spoken woman, true, and he was an eminently reasonable man. But mixed with love, well, love was neither serene nor reasonable. The way he felt now was proof enough of that.

Logan's unspoken plan to shower her with care and consideration made Catherine quietly miserable. She appreciated his attention, of course, but if she could have felt it was prompted by anything other than his inherent good manners and an absorbing interest in his soon-to-be child, she would have appreciated it a whole lot more.

She told herself she should be glad he was so interested in his potential offspring when so many expectant fathers weren't. She told herself she should be pleased he'd felt it necessary to take a "fathers only" parenting class so he'd be prepared to take his turn with diapering and bathing the baby. She told herself she should be tickled pink with the way he immediately searched out the latest nonsexist toys and books after they'd discussed her theories on childrearing, and the way he tuned in *Sesame Street* on Saturday mornings to get a feel for what their child would eventually be watching, and the way he read every baby book the doctor recommended.

And she *was* pleased. She really was!

She also resented it like hell.

And then, of course, felt small and guilty, like the most unappreciative wife and unfit mother-to-be in the world.

But just once, she thought, *just once, I wish he'd do something just for me!*

The beautifully refinished antique rocking chair he'd bought for the nursery didn't count. Neither did the silly maternity T-shirt with Baby On Board printed across the front, or the special tamales he went out of his way to get for her from the little Mexican restaurant near her old L.A. house because she casually mentioned she'd been craving them, or even the beautiful hand-carved cradle he'd proudly taken out from behind the couch in his mother's beautifully decorated living room and placed in front of the Christmas tree.

They were all for the *pregnant* her. The mother-to-be. If she hadn't been carrying his child, she reasoned, he wouldn't have bought them.

"Well," he said, watching her run her hand over the smooth wooden headboard of the cradle. "What do you think?"

"It's lovely. Really lovely, Logan." Made of pale golden oak, carved with almost Shaker-like simplicity and polished to a satiny finish, it was a beautiful, heirloom quality cradle. "I love it." *So why do I feel like crying?* "The baby will love it, too," she added, blinking back tears.

Logan was by her side immediately, crouching next to her where she knelt in front of the Christmas tree. "Catherine?" She'd been weepy lately, which the books and the doctor had warned him was normal, but her tears always concerned him, anyway. He couldn't get over the feeling she was crying because of something he'd done—or forgotten to do.

"It's nothing." She shook her head, her eyes closed to stop the threatened waterworks. "Just some of those overactive hormones Dr. Kelson warned us about." She looked up at her husband, smiling through the unshed tears that shimmered in her eyes. "It's just that it's so beautiful and I—" she brushed at an escaping tear with a fingertip "—I love it," she said truthfully.

Logan smiled gently and wiped an errant tear from her cheek with the ball of his thumb. "I'm almost afraid to give you your other presents," he said softly, wishing he dared to kiss her tears away instead; Catherine hadn't just been drawing away from his embraces these last two weeks, she'd turned away completely. He desperately hoped it was only another symptom of her pregnancy. "You might drown us all."

"There's more?" Maybe it was perfume or tickets to the ballet or a sexy nightgown to wear *after* the baby was born.

"Much more." Fiona, regally ensconced upon the lilac satin sofa beside Irene, motioned toward the tree. "You don't think he bought all those for your mother and me, do you?"

Catherine's eyes widened. "Those are all for me?" Surely, somewhere among all those packages was *something* that said he thought of her as a separate person, someone important to him apart from the life growing inside her.

"Most of them." Logan was relieved to find the books were right again; her tears were gone as easily as they'd come. He hoped her desire for him would be the same. "Here, this one's for you from Santa Claus," he said with forced joviality, handing Catherine a large, gaily wrapped package.

It was a stuffed panda with a pair of pink and blue rattles dangling from the tartan ribbon around its neck.

"And this one."

Three pastel maternity T-shirts with more silly sayings on them.

"And this one."

Every baby-name book available.

"And this one."

An exquisitely painted porcelain mother-and-child figurine from Spain by Lladro.

"And this one."

A garment bag and matching, fully stocked overnight case for the hospital—comb, brush and hand mirror, a cosmetic bag full of sample-size toiletries, butterscotch Life Savers, stationery and stamps, and two soft cotton nightgowns with matching bed jackets. One was light blue with a narrow ruffle around the neckline and tiny puff sleeves, the other was rose-sprigged white eyelet with pink ribbons threaded through the shoulder straps.

"The salesgirl said they'd be perfect for nursing," Logan said, pointing out the fact that both of them unfastened down the front. He turned back to the tree as Catherine gently folded them back into the overnight case. "This is the last one," he warned her, handing her a long, slim box.

Jewelry? she wondered, fingering the gold-and-silver wrapping. Jewelry was a very personal gift, wasn't it? Something a man gave to a woman because she *was* a woman? Or did they make jewelry for babies now?

"This is for you, Irene." He handed a similar package to his mother-in-law with a fond smile before reaching for another one. "And for the other grandmother-to-be," he said, handing the third one to Fiona.

She snatched it from his hand like a greedy child. "I hope it's terribly expensive," she said, shaking the package beside her ear. "It might help to make up for becoming a grandmother—" she shot a disgruntled look at her grinning son "—before my time. Not that I mind, my dear," she said, smiling at Catherine. "I've been waiting for this son of mine to— Oh, how exquisite!" She lifted a sparkling amethyst-and-diamond necklace to the light. "Such a clever boy." She smiled at her son. "How did you know?" she asked, as if she weren't wearing the matching earrings he'd bought her for her last birthday.

Irene's gift was a triple strand of milky pearls. "Thank you, Logan," she said, smiling as she clasped them around her neck. "They're lovely."

Eagerly, hopefully, Catherine opened her present. "Oh, Logan!" she sighed, her fingers trembling as she lifted it out of the velvet-lined box. A large, square-cut emerald flanked by a smaller pair of diamonds glittered on a long delicate silver chain. "Oh, Logan," she said again. "It's beautiful."

And personal. Something a man would give to a wife he thought of as a woman as well as the mother-to-be of his child.

"I don't know how to thank you," she said, smiling up at him with her eyes as well as her lips.

Logan smiled back. He'd finally pleased her. Really pleased her. He wasn't sure how, exactly, but he had. And that was all that mattered. "It's a sort of premother's necklace," he said.

"A what?"

"You know, like a mother's ring with her children's birthstones? I looked at rings but I thought you'd like a necklace better." He'd liked it better because all he could think about when he saw it was how it would look nestled against the creamy skin of her generous cleavage.

Catherine's smile stayed as brilliant as ever but the light in her eyes grew dimmer with each word he spoke. *A mother's necklace!* He'd given her a *mother's necklace!*

"You can exchange it for a ring if you'd like," he offered blandly, knowing he'd said something wrong. Again. He always seemed to be doing or saying something wrong these days. But damned if he knew what it was!

"Oh, no, it's beautiful." Catherine's eyes were on the pendant dangling from her fingers, so she didn't see the puzzled hurt in his. "Really beautiful."

"Indeed it is," Irene said briskly, her blue eyes darting back and forth between her daughter and son-in-law. "You've been much too generous with my girl, Logan. With all of us."

"Speak for yourself," Fiona said. Her brows lifted inquiringly as Irene got to her feet. "Where are you going?"

"Coffee's cold." Irene picked up two cups from the coffee table. "And I, for one, need a bit of refreshment before we get on with the rest of this orgy of present opening. Get those two, will you, Catherine?" she said to her daughter as she turned toward the kitchen.

"I'll get—" Logan began.

"I can do it," Catherine said, getting to her feet with the help of the coffee table. She grabbed the two cups, wanting—*needing*—to get away from her husband before she broke down in tears and demanded that he love her. "I can use the exercise," she said, following her mother out of the room and down the hall to the copper-hung kitchen.

The smell of roasting turkey and country ham filled the air. Covered pans, full of peeled, sliced potatoes, rum-spiced carrot coins and French-sliced green beans, sat on the eight-burner industrial-size stove, ready to be cooked when the time was right. Homemade yeast rolls sat on a cookie sheet, rising beautifully in the gentle heat of the room. Without looking, Catherine knew she'd find three kinds of pies—pumpkin, lemon meringue and chocolate silk—already made and waiting in the subzero refrigerator. Fiona was expecting an even dozen guests to share their Christmas dinner.

Irene placed the cups she was carrying on the tiled counter and turned to her daughter. "Do you want to talk about it?" she asked, taking the two delicate china cups Catherine held to put them down beside the others.

Catherine shrugged and, head down, rubbed her fingertip over a nonexistent spot on the counter. "Nothing to talk about," she mumbled.

"A whole lot of nothing, I'd say," said her mother.

Catherine shrugged again.

Irene put her hand out and lifted her daughter's chin. "What's wrong between you and Logan, Catherine?"

"Nothing." Tears welled but didn't fall. "Everything. Oh, I don't know!" She pulled away from her mother's touch and turned, pacing to the long, multipaned French doors that looked out over the rose garden. "It's just pregnant-lady hormones, I guess," she said, rubbing her upper arms with the opposite hands in a soothing gesture. "I get all weepy and temperamental lately for no reason at all."

"Logan may believe that but I don't, not for a minute. You haven't got a temperamental bone in your body."

"Pregnancy changes things."

"Not that much."

"No," Catherine agreed wearily, "not that much." She dropped her hands and turned to face her mother. "Giving him time hasn't worked," she said, reminding Irene of the motherly advice she'd given Catherine on her wedding day. "Being there for him hasn't worked." She put her hand on her stomach. "Even giving him babies hasn't worked. He doesn't love me, Mom—not the way a man should love his wife—and I don't know what to do."

"Catherine Marie Fletcher, that man's crazy about you!"

Catherine shook her head. "Crazy about the baby."

"It isn't the baby he's treating like a queen," Irene pointed out reasonably. "It isn't the baby he's pampering and catering to. It's you."

"Because of the baby," Catherine said stubbornly. "Couldn't you see it?" she added when Irene started to refute her. "Every present was for the baby, every—"

"Even a man who wants a child as much as Logan does isn't going to give an unborn baby an emerald necklace."

"That's just my point. An *emerald* necklace. You heard him— *Like a mother's ring with her children's birthstones.* Emeralds are the birthstone for May, when the baby will be born. If he'd really meant it for me it would have been *my* birthstone."

"Maybe you are getting a bit temperamental." Irene shook her head, a fond expression in her eyes as she looked at her daughter. "Or, at least, a little irrational."

"I know what I know," Catherine insisted. "Logan is just being—" she groped for a word "—just being *polite* to me because I'm the mother of his child. His feelings don't go any deeper than that."

"How do you know they don't go any deeper than that?" Irene asked. "Have you asked him?"

"I don't have to ask him." She was afraid to ask him. "I can tell by the way he acts."

"Talk to him," Irene advised. "Tell him how you feel. Tell him—" She paused as a thought occurred to her. "You *have* told him you love him, haven't you?"

"Not in so many words." Saying the words would drive him farther away than he was now.

"Well, then," Irene said, exasperated. "How can you expect a man like Logan to come out with it first? He doesn't trust any emotion overmuch, you know that, let alone something as 'irrational' as love." She smiled a little as she used her son-in-law's favorite adjective to describe the emotion. "He's got to feel secure in *your* love before he says the words." She turned to open the stainless-steel door of the restaurant-size freezer, satisfied the problem troubling her daughter and son-in-law could be easily solved.

"You tell him," she said over her shoulder as she took a bag of coffee beans out of the freezer, "and then come and tell me he doesn't love you."

Catherine nodded but she knew she wouldn't do it. Asking him would just be asking for trouble. Besides, she already knew how he felt about her. He'd let her know, quite clearly, without speaking a word at all. He hadn't made love to her since the Baileys' Christmas party, over two weeks ago.

* * *

In January they celebrated Logan's forty-first birthday
with his favorite Italian dish for dinner and a chocolate cake
for dessert. Catherine gave him a sophisticated pocket-size
computer with programs for an address file, memo minder
and daily calendar. She'd agonized over the gift for days,
debating whether to get him something personal, something that only a wife or lover would give a man, or something expensive but impersonal like the gifts he'd given her
for Christmas. Not that his gifts to her had been impersonal, exactly, but they hadn't been *personal*, either. They'd
been the kind of gifts a man would give to his pregnant wife.
So she gave him the pocket computer afraid he'd see something more intimate as the declaration of love it would be.

In late February she had an ultrasound test. At almost six
and a half months into her pregnancy, she was larger than
normal.

"Not abnormally large," her doctor was fast to assure
her. "Just larger than I expected. You might be carrying
twins—" Logan's paternal grandmother had been a twin
"—and, in the absence of two distinct heartbeats, ultrasound is a way to confirm or deny it."

Logan insisted on going with her, of course. He insisted
on accompanying her to every doctor's appointment but at
least before he'd stayed in the waiting room until the physical examination was over, joining her and the doctor only
during the consultation. This time he wanted to be there
from the very beginning.

Not that she didn't want him there. One part of her
wanted him there very much. But another part of her felt
distinctly uncomfortable with the idea of him seeing her
even partially undressed.

Her uneasiness with the casual familiarity of day-to-day
living and the unavoidable intimacies of married life had
begun shortly after she'd realized he hadn't made love to

her—hadn't even *tried* to make love to her—since the
Baileys' party. She'd started getting big about then, really
big, and she wasn't sure if his restraint was just one more
example of his damnable consideration for her "delicate
condition" or if her rapidly changing body turned him off.
She was desperately afraid it was the latter because, if he
loved her, the way she looked wouldn't matter. Not to either
of them.

If she knew he loved her, she could have wallowed in the
pleasure of the foot massages he offered instead of telling
him her feet were ticklish so he wouldn't see how fat and
unattractive water retention had made her ankles. She could
have stayed in the bedroom at night when she rubbed vitamin E oil into the stretched skin of her stomach, maybe even
let him rub it in for her, if he wanted to, instead of hiding in
the bathroom so he wouldn't see her swollen body. She
could have cuddled up to him in bed, secure in the knowledge that her burgeoning belly, protruding navel and dark-
ening nipples weren't any more distasteful to him than they
were to her.

If she knew he loved her, she might have even been able
to make the first sexual advances if he were too considerate
of her "delicate condition" to make them himself. As it was,
though, any baring of her body, any chance glimpse he
caught of her unclothed, made her want to run and hide
herself.

So it was with a great deal of mixed feelings that she con-
templated appearing in front of him in nothing more than
a pastel flowered hospital gown and her gym socks.

The examining room was dim, for which Catherine was
grateful, even if it was for the doctor's convenience and not
the patient's comfort. The obstetrician—a mother of two
who believed in informed patients and hands-on doctor-
ing—helped Logan to assist her up onto the examining ta-

ble. Catherine felt like a cow being hoisted onto the bed of a truck.

"I know you're uncomfortable, lying on your back like that, but just take slow, deep breaths and you'll do fine," the doctor instructed, deftly arranging a mint-green modesty drape over Catherine's legs and hips as she spoke. "You can stand right there," she said to Logan, indicating a place near Catherine's head. "Just hold her hand and help her lift her head and shoulders a little if she has trouble breathing."

"Trouble breathing?" Logan demanded suspiciously. Nobody had said anything about trouble breathing before this.

"At this stage of pregnancy, laying flat on your back puts pressure on the lungs," the doctor explained. She rolled Catherine's examining gown up, and reached for a container on the instrument tray. "The gel I'm going to use is a conductor to help me get the best picture possible. It won't hurt but I'm afraid it's going to be cold." She smiled encouragingly at her patient. "Ready?"

Catherine bit her bottom lip, glancing up at her husband as she did so. He stood to her left, slightly bent over, his arm already in position on the examining table behind her head in case she needed to be lifted to ease her breathing. He was staring at her stomach, an expression of rapt attention on his handsome face.

Fascination? Catherine wondered, feeling like a beached, bloated whale. *Or revulsion?*

Amazing, he was thinking. *Simply amazing.* It was the first time he'd actually seen her stomach like this, out in the open so to speak, with no nightgown or hastily raised towel to obstruct his view. It was beautiful and scary and awesome. He couldn't stop staring. He wanted, badly, to reach out and touch it.

"Catherine?" Dr. Kelson prompted.

"Oh, sorry." Catherine brought her gaze back to the doctor. "Yes, I'm ready."

The clear, colorless gel *was* cold. Icy cold. Catherine flinched as the obstetrician spread it over her stomach.

"Are you all right?" Logan demanded. His arm tightened around her shoulders protectively.

"Steady," Dr. Kelson murmured.

"Yes, I'm fine," Catherine assured them.

"I'm going to press this—" the obstetrician held up a flattish instrument so Catherine could see it "—against your stomach. Not hard but quite firmly, and I'll move it around very slowly to get as complete a picture as possible. You'll feel quite a bit of pressure, more so when I get near your bladder, but nothing unbearable. Let me know immediately if it hurts. Okay?"

"Okay," Catherine said, even though she wasn't sure about the "nothing unbearable" part, especially near the bladder. As instructed, she'd swallowed as much water as she could hold before the appointment and hadn't gone near a bathroom in several hours. A full bladder, she'd been told, helped push the baby up for a better picture. The pressure she was feeling now was already about as intense as she wanted it to get.

Dr. Kelson placed the instrument on her belly. "Ready?"

Catherine nodded. "Ready."

"Ready," Logan echoed, as intent as Catherine on what was about to happen.

The doctor didn't have to tell either of them to watch the small video screen placed to the right of the examining table but she did, anyway. "Remember now, we can't always get a clear enough picture to tell positively if you're carrying twins or not," she said as she moved the ultrasound instrument over Catherine's stomach. "It all depends on how the baby, or babies, are positioned. It's always possible that one is obstructing the other, in which case the results would be inconclusive and we'd have to do it again later. We're in luck here, though," she added after a moment. "We've got as clear a picture as I've ever seen."

Briefly Catherine's gaze lifted to her doctor's face.

Dorothy Kelson grinned. "I know it looks like a blur to you but that's your baby. See there? That's the umbilical cord."

Two pairs of eyes strained to make sense of the flickering grayish images on the screen. Logan's right arm was tight around Catherine's shoulders now, holding her head up a bit so she could see without straining her neck. Their left hands were tightly clasped, though neither of them was aware of it, their matching gold wedding bands glinting dully in the dim light.

"That's the spine, there. See it?" Dr. Kelson tapped the screen with her finger. "And the head." She glanced at the two rapt faces at the opposite end of the examining table. Both of them wore the same intent expression, like students trying to make sense of a diagram the teacher had drawn on the blackboard. "Think of the shape of a jumbo shrimp and you might be able to see it better."

Catherine frowned at the description, then decided the doctor was right. The flickering image did look something like a shrimp, large at the head, smaller as it curled down toward the feet, but it didn't matter. It was her baby. The bond that had begun forming the moment she realized she was pregnant became a hundred times stronger in an instant.

That's my baby! My baby! She felt overwhelmed. Ecstatic. Blessed.

"Do you want to know the sex?" Dr. Kelson asked.

"Can you really tell?" Catherine asked, her eyes never leaving the screen.

"From this angle, yes, without a doubt."

Catherine tore her gaze away from the screen to look up at her husband. "Logan?"

When he looked at her, his eyes were as blurred with tears as her own. He'd never felt so overwhelmed, so awed, so close to the woman held securely in the curve of his right arm. That was their baby up there on that screen! His and Catherine's. A miracle. "Yes."

"Yes," Catherine said to Dr. Kelson.

"You're sure?"

"Yes," they both said at the same time.

"I hope you have lots of blue." Dorothy Kelson tapped the screen again to show them the proof. "It's a boy."

"A boy," they echoed together, like two worshipers chanting at a sacred shrine. Without planning or hesitation, they turned to each other and kissed. It was a hard, joyous, exuberant kiss—the first truly spontaneous gesture they'd made toward each other in months.

Catherine's happy tears spilled over as she turned her fascinated gaze back to the screen. "We're going to have a baby boy," she whispered.

"A son," Logan agreed, blinking back his own tears of joy.

Just then, the image seemed to roll and a foot—surely it was a foot!—extended outward. At the same time, Catherine felt a strong nudge from inside and her belly jutted out just to the left of her navel. Without thinking, she yanked Logan's left hand down and pressed it flat against the bump made by their son's tiny foot. Neither one of them paid any attention to the clear goo spread over her stomach or the doctor standing with the ultrasound instrument pressed against Catherine's stomach.

"Feel him?" she whispered excitedly. "There, he did it again. Feel?"

Logan's eyes were wide as they left the screen to stare down at his wife. "He's so strong," he whispered, amazed and delighted and nearer to crying than he'd ever been in his life. "Does it hurt?"

Catherine smiled and shook her head, her gaze never leaving Logan's. She'd never felt closer or more connected to anyone in her life. It was as if, for that brief moment, they shared the same soul. "Just a little love tap to let us know he's there," she said softly, looking at her husband with love in her eyes.

But he'd already turned his head to look at the ultrasound screen again.

Seven

It wasn't until the middle of March that Catherine began to suspect Logan had fallen in love with another woman. She'd predicted it would happen on the day he proposed to her, waited for it, dreaded it, and now he'd actually done it. If it weren't for baby Zac—Zacariah Logan Fletcher, that's what they'd decided to name him—she thought she might just curl up and die from the pain.

But she had her baby to think about now, her baby to love. It didn't make Logan's... Her mind groped for a word. Desertion? Yes, that's what it felt like even though he hadn't left her yet and, given his sterling character and sense of responsibility, probably never would. But it was, she decided, desertion nonetheless.

Having the baby to look forward to didn't make it easier—nothing could make losing Logan easier—but it did make it bearable. Just.

It had hurt when he'd turned away from her in bed after she'd started to show, as if, now that the desired result had been achieved, he no longer wanted her. It had wounded her to the core when he stopped offering her even the casual, quick kisses and caresses-in-passing he'd shared with her in the early days of their marriage. It smote her to her very soul when he started avoiding her altogether.

Not that he was cruel about it. Or even obvious. He was still unfailingly polite, kissing her when he left for work each morning and again when he came home at night. He was still conscientious, thanking her for any little thing she did for him, accompanying her to the doctor, making sure the special little pillow she used to ease her constant backache was always within reach. He was still considerate and understanding and so kind she wanted to scream.

More and more, he stayed late at the office, first, of course, conscientiously calling to let her know he wouldn't be home for dinner. "Tax time," he'd say, as if the fact he was the accountant/investor/asset manager for Fletcher, Bailey and Webb was the real reason for his absence.

She might have believed him except that even when he *was* home, he wasn't there. She'd look at him, sitting at the opposite end of the sofa from her, supposedly engrossed in the latest *Wall Street Journal* or *Variety* or a thick tax code book, but he was really miles away. He'd have this unfocused, faraway, mooning, mournful look in his eyes and she'd know.

He was thinking about *her*. The other woman. The woman who had, at last, sparked his dormant capacity for love and led him into his "grand affair."

By the first week in April, Catherine was sure she knew who the woman was. Not, of course, that she didn't already have a strong suspicion. She'd called Logan's office one evening around seven o'clock to ask him to stop by the drugstore on the way home and pick up a giant-size bottle of vitamin E oil. All through their brief conversation she could hear the low, sultry, familiar laugh of a woman in the background.

What's he doing, she wondered miserably, *tickling her while he talks to me?*

After that the woman had gotten bolder. She'd actually called him at home one Saturday morning, supposedly in a panic over a letter from the Internal Revenue Service.

"Meet me at my office around, oh, eleven-thirty, Dee," he'd said, glancing at his watch. "The letter's got to be a mistake. You didn't make enough last year to owe that much." His laugh had been intimate. "Unless you've been holding out on me."

Holding out on him, ha! Catherine thought. *She's probably been giving it to him on a silver platter!*

Politely, perfunctorily, he'd asked his wife if she'd like to come with him; he'd drop her off at Barbara Bailey's on his way in and he'd pick her up on the way back.

He knew I'd say no, she thought furiously. At eight weeks and counting, she didn't go anywhere she didn't have to, and he knew it. When she repeated her refusal, he'd kissed her on the cheek, told her not to wait dinner for him and all but ran out the door in his eagerness to go to his lady love.

To Deirdre Walsh.

Television's newest sex goddess.

Emmy award winner for Best Supporting Actress in a Drama Series.

Homewrecker.

Bitch.

Catherine was so furious she didn't even cringe at her mental castigation of a woman she hardly knew. Nor did she pause to remember that Logan had been planning to go to the office even before Deirdre called because he went to the office most Saturdays from late February until the tax deadline on April 15th. It was his busiest time.

But Catherine didn't think about that.

She was too busy thinking about how she'd like to kick Deirdre Walsh's sleek little rear down Hollywood Boulevard at high noon—after she'd dragged Logan through the divorce courts and taken every blessed penny the two-timer had! She'd make sure he got limited—*very* limited—visitation, too, she thought vehemently, cradling her bulging belly. *That* would make him sorry!

How she'd love to tell him that—coldly, calmly, heartlessly—just to see the look on his face! But she knew it wouldn't happen, mainly because she'd probably break down in tears before she got it all out. And she wasn't about to give him the satisfaction of falling apart. Besides, all this useless wailing was probably bad for the baby.

By the time Logan got home that night—after 11:00 p.m.—Catherine was in perfect control. Through sheer will and the exercise of deep-seated feminine pride, she managed to put on a facade of serene indifference. If Logan didn't love her, well, it wasn't something he'd done on purpose. If he loved someone else, well, he hadn't done that on purpose, either. A man couldn't order his emotions any more than a woman could.

What mattered was that he was good to her. And he *was* good to her. He was kind and considerate, a wonderful caring provider who was going to make a wonderful caring father. Lots of women settled for far less in a husband, Catherine told herself, as if believing it would make a difference, and they still managed to be happy.

It wasn't as if anyone had lied to her—she'd known from the beginning what she was getting into. She'd known, even if he hadn't, that he was bound to fall in love sooner or later. She'd been willing to take the chance it would be with her.

Was it fair to cry "foul" now, just because she'd been wrong?

If she did that, she'd lose him for sure. And she wasn't ready—not yet, not now, maybe not ever—to lose even the small part of him she had. No, what happened had been inevitable from the beginning and she might as well accept it.

Besides, there was always the chance—if she was calm and serene and careful not to confront him with an ugly scene and screaming accusations—it would blow over. Because maybe, just maybe, what he felt for Deirdre Walsh was what he'd always said love really was. Lust.

It could happen. Even to a man as reasonable and in control of himself as Logan. After all, he hadn't been sharing any of his healthy virility with his wife lately. And if any woman had been fashioned to inspire lust in a man—especially a man who wasn't getting his "needs" met at home—it was Deirdre Walsh.

The bitch!

Logan hung up the phone slowly, uneasy about the tone he'd heard in Catherine's voice when she told him not to worry about missing their Lamaze class. It wasn't that she'd hollered or screeched or even been annoyed with him as she had every right to be. She had, in fact, sounded as calm and serene and unruffled as she had at any other time in the last four and a half months.

"It won't matter if we miss the last class," she'd said pleasantly. "It'll probably just be a review. Besides, people have been having babies for thousands of years without taking classes first."

He couldn't ask for a more understanding wife but, still, there was something.... He shook his head and went back to the ledger sheets spread out in front of him.

The thing was, he thought, throwing his pencil down to run a hand through his hair, there was *always* something in

Catherine's voice lately. Something vaguely... Vaguely what? He'd have said martyred if it'd been anyone else, but Catherine didn't play the martyr. Hurt? Was that it? Maybe, but for the life of him he couldn't think of anything he might have said or done to hurt her feelings.

Even her supersensitive, hormone-skewed feelings.

"God, I can't wait until the baby's born," he muttered.

"What's that?" Barnaby Webb, a C.P.A. as well as a brilliant entertainment lawyer, was working on the other side of the littered conference table. Ned, who wouldn't recognize a tax credit if it walked and introduced itself, and the rest of the staff had already gone home.

"Just wishing out loud," Logan said. "Two weeks and six days till the Due Date." He said the last two words as if they were of global significance.

Barnaby pushed his glasses up on his nose. "I take it your wife's getting impatient."

"Yeah." Logan raised his arms above his head in a bone-cracking stretch. "We both are."

And that, he thought as he picked up his pencil again, *must surely qualify as the understatement of the year.*

He wasn't just impatient, he was chomping at the bit, foaming at the mouth, rarin' to go, in a virtual sweat... all the clichés applied. If the baby wasn't born soon he was going to go out of what little mind he had left!

It was still a source of surprise to him that his impatience wasn't solely connected with seeing his son for the first time. It was partly that, of course—he was dying to welcome his son into the world—but, mostly, it was the thought of finally getting Catherine... *Back,* was the word that popped into his mind.

Which was pretty funny, considering he'd never really had her in the first place.

He sighed at the glum realization. No, she'd never really been his. Not completely. Not the way he wanted her to be.

But she could be, he thought, cheering up a little. He was *sure* she could be. And soon, very soon, he'd know for certain. He'd give her a few weeks—five, six, whatever the doctor recommended—to recover from childbirth and then watch out! He was going to let it all out, hit her with both barrels as it were, and let her know exactly—no pussyfooting around, no skirting the edges of the issue, no timid euphemisms to protect his pride in case she turned him down but *exactly*—how he felt.

These past few months of holding himself on an emotional leash had been pure, unadulterated hell!

"Is it worth it?" Barnaby asked, seemingly out of the blue.

Logan looked up from the ledger sheet he'd been scowling at for the past five minutes. "Huh?"

"Was it worth it?"

Logan looked back at the ledger sheet as if whatever Barnaby was referring to had something to do with the tax statements they were working on. "Was what worth it?"

Barnaby colored slightly. "Being responsible to someone else. Losing your, uh—" he paused, visibly uncomfortable, as always, with discussing personal matters "—your freedom?"

"My freedom?"

"You know. Marriage."

"Oh." A slow smile spread over Logan's face as understanding dawned. "I take it Dee's putting the pressure on."

"No, it's not— Yeah," Barnaby admitted sheepishly, "Deirdre's putting the pressure on. She said, and I quote, 'It's time to fish or cut bait.'" He shook his head, looking like a hound dog who couldn't understand why his master wouldn't let him sleep on the bed anymore. "I thought everything was going along just fine," he said. "I was happy. I thought she was happy. But now—" he paused to push his glasses up on his nose "—she said to come back when I decide what I want and if it's not commitment, then don't come back at all."

"Kicked you out of bed, did she?" Logan said sympathetically. It was easy to be sympathetic. He knew exactly how his partner felt.

Barnaby blushed like a teenager whose mother had just confronted him with a girlie magazine she'd found under his bed. "Yeah," he murmured.

"And you want back in."

Barnaby's blush deepened as he nodded.

Logan couldn't help but grin. Barnaby was thirty-five years old, a shrewd, highly successful entertainment lawyer with an M.B.A. and his C.P.A.'s license to fall back on in case the legal profession ever went bust. He was good-looking in that cool, understated, upper-crust way that showed generations of superior breeding. He was also as shy as a schoolboy about women.

"Repressed," as Deirdre had said. And then she'd grinned. "But I'll loosen him up."

It looked to Logan as if she'd succeeded. Barnaby had gone way beyond "loosened" all the way to shaken. Badly. As a fellow sufferer, Logan empathized completely. Being in love was hell.

"How much do you want her?" Logan asked.

"I think about her all the time," Barnaby said miserably. "I can't eat. I can't sleep." He swept his arm out over the table. "I can't even work, dammit!"

"Well, in that case, I'd say you've got two choices."

"Which are?"

"Marry her or—" he held up his hand to keep Barnaby from speaking "—or make her fall so much in love with you she'll take you back even without a commitment."

Barnaby snorted. "Yeah, right." He looked across the table with a hangdog, hopeful expression on his face. "Any idea how I accomplish that?"

Logan had lots of ideas. Tons of them. A whole truck-load. Thinking of ways to make a woman fall in love with a particular man had occupied most of his waking hours lately. And maybe even some of his sleeping ones.

"Romance," he said sagely. "Flowers. Soft music. Champagne. Candlelight. All that stuff. Women love it." He knew because he'd asked around. Discreetly, of course, because he still felt uncomfortable admitting he was in love with his wife to anyone but himself. Given his record of un-complicated, uninvolved relationships with the opposite sex, no one would believe him anyway. He still had a hard time believing it.

"So?" Barnaby said.

"So send her a dozen roses for no reason." Roses had al-ways worked on Fiona. "Send her a singing telegram or a balloon bouquet or a giant stuffed teddy bear." One of the secretaries had grinned for days when her boyfriend did that. "Take her to dinner at her favorite restaurant. Bring her breakfast in bed and make damn sure her favorite flower's on the tray." The last was something he'd thought of all on his own.

"Deirdre took back the key to her house."

"Then write her a love letter. Send her cards—silly cards, romantic cards, whatever—so she has to think of you every day. Write poetry." He had a few romantic verses of his own he intended to use if he had to. "Grovel at her feet for being such an insensitive idiot," he said expansively, warming to his subject. "Beg her forgiveness for not realizing how much you loved her sooner. Hell, man, make a complete fool of yourself over her if that's what it takes." It was what he was planning to do when the time was right. He'd observed that women loved it when men made fools of themselves. "Talk to her. Be there when she needs you." He was talking to himself now, barely aware that Barnaby was even in the room. "Don't let a day go by without letting her know how much she means to you."

"It'd be easier to get married," Barnaby mumbled.

But Logan wasn't listening. He stood abruptly, reaching for his jacket on the back of the chair, and headed for the door without saying goodbye to his flabbergasted partner.

How late did flower shops stay open at night?

Catherine looked at the roses he brought her as if she thought they might be hiding a black widow spider. "How thoughtful," she said, smiling as she reluctantly took them from him. *And how appropriate.* A dozen red roses—long stemmed, hot-house fragile, extravagantly expensive—were the time-honored, traditional offering of a guilty man. He'd probably spent the hours between five and—she glanced at the wall clock—eight-thirty on the sofa in his office, making wild, passionate love to Deirdre Walsh. "I'll just put them in water before they wilt," she said, turning away from him to put them in the sink.

What she'd like to do is stuff them down the garbage disposal—and him after them!

"Would you get a vase for me?" she said over her shoulder as she turned the water on. "They're in the bottom of the china cabinet in the dining room. The tall crystal one Ned and Barbara gave us for our wedding," she said, subtly reminding him he was a married man. *As if it would do any good at this late date!*

She was carefully, savagely snipping the ends of the stems off under running water when he brought the vase in to her. "Just set it on the counter, right there," she said, inclining her head without turning around.

He lingered behind her, wondering what he'd done wrong now, trying to think of something to do that would make it right.

"Why don't you go take a shower," she suggested. *Wash off the stench of your lover.* "I've already eaten—" it was a gentle rebuke, as deadly sharp as a dart "—but there's some leftover enchiladas I can warm up." She placed the long-stemmed roses into the crystal vase as precisely as if she were a picador plunging the short, decorated lances into the shoulder of a bull. "It'll be ready by the time you finish showering."

"I thought Mexican food gave you heartburn these days," he said, because he didn't know what else to say.

What he wanted to say couldn't be said. Not yet. Not when she was standing there, nearly as wide as she was tall these days, her feet angled outward like a duck's and leaning slightly backward to balance the weight of the child in her womb. To confront her now, to grasp her by the shoulders and turn her around and demand that she look at him, really look at him, would probably bring on premature labor. Then she'd really have a reason to be mad at him.

"We could still make the Lamaze class if we hurry," he said, trying to placate her. He should have known a mere offering of sixty-dollar roses wouldn't do it. "I could grab a hamburger on the way home. And you could have an order of fries," he said coaxingly.

She'd developed a craving for French fries in the past week or so, as fierce as the craving she'd had for Mexican food from the beginning of her pregnancy. They both gave her heartburn but, hell, she'd apparently had enchiladas for dinner so the damage was already done.

"You know Dr. Kelson said I should try to watch my weight," she said, somehow managing to sound as if he were deliberately torturing her by suggesting the forbidden food. She placed the last rose in the vase and stepped back from the sink. "There, that's done." She reached for the dish towel and wiped her hands as if they'd had something nasty on them. "They'll look lovely on the dining-room table."

Where I won't have to look at them too often. "Would you take them in there for me, please?" She turned toward the refrigerator.

Logan stood where he was. "Catherine?"

"Do you want a salad with your enchiladas?"

"Catherine, look at me."

"Hmm-mm?"

He put his hand on her shoulder and gently turned her around, reaching past her with his free hand to close the refrigerator door. "Do you want to go to that Lamaze class or not?"

"I've already called and canceled." She held the pan of enchiladas in one hand and a tomato in the other, speaking, not impatiently, he decided, but as if she just couldn't take the time to stop and talk to him right now.

His hand tightened fractionally, holding her. "You could call and uncancel."

"It's not important," she said, deftly slipping out from under his hand. He was being kind again, humoring the pregnant lady, and she couldn't stand it. "The instructor said it would just be a review of what we've already learned, like I thought." She set the pan of enchiladas on the stove. "Now—" she hefted the tomato in her hand, directing his attention to it "—do you want a salad with your dinner?"

Logan sighed. "Yes, thank you, a salad would be fine," he said politely, turning toward the door as he spoke. "I'll go take that shower."

Catherine barely restrained herself from throwing the tomato at the back of his head.

Eight

―――

Only ten days to go, Catherine consoled herself as she stood in the middle of her walk-in closet in her bare feet and Logan's old terry bathrobe, trying to find something comfortable—meaning big enough—to wear. Only ten more days, give or take a few, and then not every scrap of clothing she owned would be too small. Just about three-fourths of it still wouldn't fit.

"Don't throw away your maternity clothes just yet," Dorothy Kelson warned her at the last appointment. "Especially the pants. They're going to be the only thing that's comfortable for the first few weeks."

"Wonderful," Catherine said aloud, scowling at the lavender floral print maternity dress she'd just taken off the closet rod. A gift from Fiona, it was sleeveless with a narrow ruffle at the high, round neck and a deeper one around the midcalf hem. Too ruffly by half for her taste. And too...purple.

Would the good doctor care if she showed up for her appointment in Logan's bathrobe?

Probably not, Catherine decided, smiling to herself. Dorothy Kelson had two children of her own and she understood the adjustments and discomforts of pregnancy as no male obstetrician ever could. *But I'd mind.*

Logan still insisted on accompanying her to every doctor's appointment even though they were hardly more than excruciatingly polite roommates now. As long as it was in her power, he wasn't going to see her looking any worse than she could help. She was going to go on being serene and calm, capable and uncomplaining—all the things, in fact, that he'd married her for—even if it killed her. It was to that end that she'd refused to have him drive from his office back up into the hills where their house was located to pick her up for the doctor's appointment.

"I'm pregnant, Logan, not infirm," she'd told him. "I can still drive a car."

Not comfortably, of course. She could barely move once she was behind the wheel but Logan didn't have to know that.

Sighing, she hung the lavender floral dress back on the closet rod and reached for "old faithful," one of two light cotton denim jumpers she'd bought in her seventh month and worn interchangeably—and nearly exclusively—since then. Worn over a blue-and-white striped jersey T-shirt with red leather flip-flops on her feet—anything that had to be laced was out of the question—and a narrow red ribbon holding her hair off her face, she was at least cool and comfortable.

If comfortable was a word that could be used in reference to a woman in the last ten days of pregnancy.

Catherine sighed again, sure it wasn't, and surveyed herself in the wall mirror. The baby'd dropped two days ago, causing her to lean even farther backward to counteract the weight, and intensifying her constant backache.

She smoothed her hands over and under the bulge of her belly, noting with pleasure how long and strong her nails had gotten in the past eight months and twenty days. Her hands, at least, were beautiful. And her hair. It had gotten longer and thicker, too, swinging against her shoulders when she turned her head. She patted it into place, enjoying the silky feel of it, then dropped her hand quickly, covering her mouth against the tiny burp that rose in her throat.

The tacos with salsa for dinner last night had probably been a bad idea.

Well, in another ten days it'd be all over. She patted her belly lovingly. "And it will have all been worth it."

The guard at the entrance to the underground parking lot recognized her immediately, waving her inside without requiring her to stop and identify herself. She pulled into a parking space under the towering, copper-glass skyscraper and struggled out from behind the wheel of her Mercedes station wagon. It took a full minute of concentrated wriggling, and then she had to lean back in, balancing her hand on the back of the seat to keep from toppling over, to get her purse.

The walk to the elevator seemed longer than usual, the express elevator to the two floors that housed Fletcher, Bailey and Webb slower, the air-conditioning less efficient than it should be. Catherine put one hand on the small of her back, arching in an effort to relieve the pressure, and dabbed at her upper lip with a Kleenex as a particularly sharp pain gripped her middle. That salsa *really* hadn't been a good idea; she'd never had heartburn so bad.

The receptionist stood as Catherine stepped off the elevator directly into the front office. She came quickly around her polished marble-topped desk and put her hand under

Catherine's elbow. "Wow, you must be really close to your time, Mrs. Fletcher," she said, smiling her perfectly polished, perfectly welcoming receptionist's smile.

She probably got an A in smiling at receptionists' school, Catherine thought sourly, knowing she was being hateful and unfair. The young woman was only being friendly. But Catherine was feeling uncharacteristically hostile toward anyone with even a hint of a waistline lately and the receptionist's tiny midsection was showcased by a fashionable high-waisted skirt and a chunky gold chain belt.

"Janice told me to tell you to go right on down as soon as you came in," the receptionist said. Janice was Logan's private secretary. "Mr. Fletcher's expecting you."

"I know where his office is, thank you." Catherine smiled sweetly as she withdrew her arm from the young woman's grasp. "I've been there before."

"Are you sure you don't need any help?" The receptionist's big brown eyes were faintly anxious as she glanced down at Catherine's belly.

"Pregnancy makes walking under my own steam difficult, I'll admit, but not impossible," Catherine said over her shoulder as she headed down the plushly carpeted hall to her husband's office.

Logan's secretary, Janice, looked up as Catherine walked into Logan's outer office. "Mrs. Fletcher," she said, coming to her feet. "Are you all right?"

"I'm fine." *What was with everybody?* "Is Logan in his office?"

"Yes, of course." She moved as if to take Catherine's arm, then drew back as if she were afraid to touch her. "Would you like to sit down while I tell him you're here?"

"No, I'll just go on in. He's expecting me."

With Janice hovering anxiously behind her, Catherine put her hand on the doorknob and pushed open the door to Logan's office. It swung back on silent, well-oiled hinges.

Catherine froze in her tracks.

Logan was standing in profile to the door, his head bent, his arms around Deirdre Walsh. The redhead was crying noisily into his shoulder.

"I'm sorry. I'm sorry," she said between sobs. "But I can't live like this anymore. I just can't."

Logan rubbed her back and told her not to cry. "It'll be all right," he said, knowing from experience that it was the only thing to say to a woman who'd been crossed in love. "You'll see." Fiona had used his shoulder for just such a purpose on countless occasions.

The sight of Deirdre Walsh in her husband's arms was the proof of every suspicion Catherine had harbored about them in the past month and a half.

Catherine reacted from pure instinct. Her body screamed fight or flight, and she was in no condition for the first. Without a word she turned, almost plowing into Janice, who'd come to a standstill behind her.

"Mrs. Fletcher," Janice said as Catherine pushed by her without a word of apology. "Are you all right?"

"Mrs. Fletcher," the receptionist echoed, jumping to her feet as Catherine stabbed the elevator button with savage, frustrated fury. "Is anything wrong?"

Catherine ignored them both, stepping into the elevator as the doors slid open.

"Catherine." She heard Logan's voice calling her name as the doors slid closed.

She ignored him, too.

Of all the two-timing, unfaithful… Logan and that…that *bitch* right there in his office! Everyone knew! Everyone *must* know! He wasn't saving his illicit lovemaking for after-hours or weekends anymore. He was flaunting her now!

Oh, God!

"I can't live like this anymore," she'd said, sobbing into her lover's comforting arms. *"I just can't."*

"Well, neither can I," Catherine said as the elevator doors opened, depositing her in the parking garage.

She hurried across the concrete floor, one hand cradled under her stomach as if to protect it, looking like a well-fed duck fleeing in panic from a hungry fox, afraid Logan would catch up with her even though none of the other elevators that stopped on his floor were express.

She squeezed herself behind the wheel of the Mercedes, fumbled with the keys and gunned the engine to life. The tires squealed as she backed out of the parking space, then left rubber on the floor as she stomped on the accelerator and shot toward the exit. The garage attendant, realizing she didn't intend to slow down, hastily raised the arm to let her out. She drove fast and furiously, swearing under her breath, tears streaming down her cheeks—a woman possessed by pain and fury.

She was no calmer when she got home. The brakes squealed as she came to a stop in the driveway. The door of the Mercedes slammed so hard the car shook. She left doors open behind her in her haste to... to what?

The phone was ringing when she reached the bedroom, shrilly demanding to be answered. She ignored it, knowing the answering machine would take the call.

Logan's voice came over the wire. "Catherine, are you there? Catherine?"

She continued to ignore it.

She wanted to tear something apart with her bare hands. She wanted to beat someone to a pulp. She wanted to break crockery into a million tiny pieces. She wanted to wreak havoc on— Her gaze fell on the two small suitcases sitting by the bedroom door. They were the ones Logan had bought for her, packed and ready for the hospital.

She picked them up, stomped across the room and flung them out of the sliding glass door onto the wooden deck. When that didn't seem like enough, she went out and kicked

them off the deck into the gaping hole that'd been dug for
their swimming pool.

"Take *that*, Logan Fletcher," she said, brushing her
hands together as she came back into the bedroom. Then she
sank onto the side of the bed and buried her face in her
hands.

She was almost nine months pregnant. Married to a man
who didn't love her. She had no job. No income. No home
except the one he'd given her, she thought dramatically. She
couldn't even go home to her mother because—she hiccuped through her tears, pressing a palm to the dull pain
below her breastbone—because her mother's home belonged to *his* mother!

What on earth was she going to do?

With an anguished wail, Catherine threw herself onto the
bed sideways and sobbed into her unfaithful husband's pillow. Ten minutes later, she choked back her tears, sitting up
as she automatically reached for the ringing telephone.

No, she thought, drawing her hand back, *it's probably
Logan again.*

She didn't want to talk to him. Not now. Maybe not ever.
Let him talk to the answering machine. She cocked her head,
listening intently as the machine clicked on and picked up
the call.

"Catherine, are you there? If you're there, pick up the
phone."

Catherine smiled at the frantic sound of his voice. *Good,*
she thought, pressing both hands to her stomach as if to
soothe an ache. *He deserves to sound frantic.*

"Catherine, dammit, if you're there *pick up the phone!*"

Catherine reached out and picked up the receiver. "You
don't have to yell, Logan. I'm not deaf."

"Are you all right?" he demanded.

"As good as can be expected under the circumstances," she replied smoothly, amazed at how calm she sounded. Her insides were boiling like a witch's caldron.

"Under the circumstances? What circumstances? What's the matter? Are you all right?"

"I'm fine." For a woman in what she was beginning to suspect were the first stages of labor, who'd also just seen with her own eyes that her husband was cheating on her, she was just dandy.

"Why did you run out of the office like that? And why aren't you at the doctor's? I drove over here like a madman, thinking that's where you were headed so fast. I thought you'd suddenly gone into labor or something."

There was a long moment of silence on Catherine's end of the line. She could use that, she thought. She could say it was labor that had driven her from his office, and pretend she'd never seen Deirdre Walsh in his arms.

"Catherine?"

They could go on just as they had been if she said she'd run because she was in labor. It would almost be the truth, too. Because she was, she realized now, definitely in labor.

"Catherine, answer me, dammit!"

"I forgot all about my doctor's appointment," she said. "It just went right out of my mind."

"Well, you scared me to death. What happened to make you act like that?"

Catherine decided on the truth. The bald, naked, painful truth. "This isn't working, Logan."

"*What* isn't working?"

"Us. The marriage."

"What the hell kind of nonsense is that?" He could feel his control slipping away from him. "What do you mean, 'it isn't working'? Why isn't it working?"

"I think you know the reason."

"I haven't got the sli—"

"I've got to hang up now, Logan. I have to get ready to go to the hospital."

"Hospital?" He sounded completely unstrung now. "You're going to the hospital?"

"Let Dr. Kelson know I've started labor, will you?" she said. "There's no hurry, though. Tell her I'll call her before I leave for the hospital."

"Labor? You mean the baby's coming *now*?" He nearly shrieked.

Catherine hung up on him.

Logan broke all speed records getting home. That the LAPD or the California Highway Patrol didn't flag him down was a minor miracle. It probably would have ended in ugly headlines in the tabloids—*Fiona Fletcher's son arrested after wild car chase*—because he wouldn't have stopped. Not for anything.

He pulled his Jag to a screeching stop beside Catherine's midnight blue Mercedes and stormed into the house, slamming the doors she'd left open in her own mad rush. He found her in the bedroom, calmly packing a suitcase. Two others lay open and half full between her and the door.

She'd said she was in labor, that the baby was coming and here she was—calmly packing every suitcase she owned!

"Just what the hell is this all about?" he roared, completely forgetting he had nothing but contempt for people who couldn't control their emotions—as well as the fact that she shouldn't be upset in her "delicate condition."

Catherine looked up from the blouse she was folding into the open suitcase. "I'm packing," she said calmly, reaching for another garment among the jumble on the bed.

"I can see that." It looked as if she intended on taking half her wardrobe to the hospital. What wasn't on the bed or in the open suitcases was draped across the backs of the two armchairs that faced the fireplace. "What the hell for?"

"It's not necessary to shout, Logan." Another neatly folded blouse joined its companions in the suitcase. "And it's not necessary to swear in every other sentence, either."

"It's necessary to me!" He stormed across the room, stepping over the open suitcases and grabbed her arm. "What in hell's going— Oh, my God!" His grip turned from restraining to supporting as she hunched her shoulders slightly. He reached for her other shoulder and gently lowered her to the edge of the bed. "How far apart are the contractions?"

"About nine or ten minutes." She leaned her forehead against his midsection, breathing slowly and deeply as she'd been taught in Lamaze class. "I think," she said, when the pain passed.

"You think? Don't you know?"

She shook her head. "It's close enough."

"Close enough? Close enough for what? Oh, never mind," he said as she opened her mouth to answer him. "We've got to get you to the hospital."

Everything else could wait for now. Even her ridiculous statement about the marriage not working.

"Here, lie down for a minute—" he pushed the suitcase off the bed, tumbling neatly folded clothes all over the floor "—while I close your suitcases and put them in the car."

"I don't want to lie down," Catherine said, resisting his efforts to lift her feet to the mattress. "I've got things to do."

"Tell me what they are," he demanded, pushing her back down. "I'll do it."

"You can't do it, Logan. I have to do it myself."

"I can do whatever you want done," he insisted.

Catherine looked at him from under her brows, her expression that of a woman thoroughly exasperated with the stupidity of men. "Preparation for childbirth, Logan," she said. "Remember our classes on 'What to do before you leave for the hospital'?"

He let her up.

"I'll finish packing for you," he said as she headed for the bathroom.

"Fine, you do that." The bathroom door slammed behind her.

Logan ran his hand through his hair. "What in hell's the matter with her?" he wondered out loud as he looked around the room. *And what in hell had she been planning to do with three big suitcases?*

He pushed aside the niggling little feeling that it just might have something to do with her statement about the marriage not working. He told himself he didn't have time to think of it right now.

He crouched, closing the two suitcases on the floor, and set them upright near her closet door, then gathered up the things that tumbled out of the one he'd pushed off the bed, and did the same to it.

Where were the pale blue leather suitcases she was supposed to take to the hospital?

They'd been packed for a month—the well-stocked overnight case he'd bought her for Christmas and the matching lightweight carryall with baby clothes and blankets and the bright blue cotton knit dress she planned to wear home from the hospital. They should have been standing by the bedroom door, ready to go at any minute of the day or night.

He tapped lightly on the bathroom door. "Where are your suitcases?" When she didn't answer, he knocked louder to make himself heard above the sound of running water. "Catherine?"

The door flew open under his hand. "What do you want?" she demanded.

Logan drew back. What was she so mad about? "Your suitcases. Where are they?"

She gestured with her toothbrush. "Right there."

"No, your packed ones. For the hospital."

"I—" What could she say? "I got rid of them."

"Got rid of them?" Logan ran a hand through his hair. "Why? Where?"

She shrugged in answer to his first question. "Outside," she said in answer to his second.

"Outside?" What were her suitcases doing outside? "Where outside? Have you already put them in the car?"

She waved an impatient hand toward the sliding glass doors that opened onto the deck, flicking toothpaste foam on the jacket of his stylish double-breasted suit. "Outside."

With a sigh, Logan strode across the room and through the open glass door. The suitcases weren't on the deck. He walked to the edge and looked down. The two leather suitcases lay in the bottom of what would eventually be their swimming pool.

What in hell's the matter with her?

She needed those suitcases. Besides her personal things and the baby's clothes, they held all the necessary items for natural childbirth. Petroleum jelly to sooth lips made dry from panting, the portable CD player with her favorite music, the decks of cards to pass the time between contractions, the little glass hummingbird for her to concentrate on during them.

He turned, storming back into the bedroom. "Good Lord, Catherine!" He jerked the bathroom door open. "What in hell did you do th—"

She was standing with a giant bath towel wrapped around her, one hand braced on the sink and the other cradling her belly, taking slow, deep breaths.

Logan rushed into the room, reaching out to steady her with an arm around her shoulders. "Okay, now, sweetheart?'' he said when she straightened. ''Contraction over?''

She nodded.

''Okay, then.'' He bent as if to lift her into his arms. ''Let's get you to the hospital.''

She struggled out of his grasp. ''For God's sake, Logan. It's not time to go to the hospital.''

''But you're in labor!''

''Just barely. The pains are only a little less than ten minutes apart. There's plenty of time.'' She pushed him away and hitched her towel up around her body. ''Now get out of here so I can take a shower.''

''You can't take a shower when you're in labor.''

She frowned at him. ''Out.''

''What if you have a contraction?''

''Then I'll stand still until it's over.''

''But—''

''Get out of here,'' she said, pointing at the door.

Logan got out.

It must be hormones, he decided.

It was the only explanation he could think of to explain her bizarre behavior.

But should she be acting so crazy quite so soon in her labor? Wasn't that something that was supposed to happen after... What was the word he wanted? *Transition?*

Well, whatever the reason, she needed those suitcases. He went back outside to the deck, jumping lightly to the ground behind it and then into what would eventually be the shallow end of the pool to retrieve them. His gray suit was smeared with the same dirty streaks as the two pale blue leather suitcases when he climbed out again.

Catherine was still in the bathroom when he carried them back inside. He could hear the shower running. He ran his hand through his hair. *What now?*

The books and childbirth classes had told Catherine what she was supposed to do to prepare for labor but they hadn't mentioned anything specific for him to do except make her "as comfortable as possible."

That was going to be a bit difficult to do if Catherine insisted on being so difficult through the whole process.

He heard the water shut off and, a few minutes later, the sound of a blow dryer told him she was fooling with her hair. "Dammit, Catherine," he muttered, sinking onto the edge of the bed. "The baby isn't going to care if your hair's done."

When she came out of the bathroom a half hour later, he was still sitting there. For a moment she considered going to him, putting her arm around his shoulders and telling him everything was going to be all right. He had such a miserable, hangdog expression on his face. But, then... *Good,* she thought, *let him suffer a little. He deserves to suffer.*

"You can call Dr. Kelson now," she said as she passed him on her way to the closet.

"You've finally decided it's time to go to the hospital?"

"As soon as I get dressed." She disappeared into the closet, leaving him to make the call. She was just finishing up the buttons on a plain white blouse when Logan hollered at her from the bedroom.

"The doctor's secretary wants to know how close your contractions are."

She pulled a clean denim jumper on over her head. "About five minutes," she called back, pulling it into place over her stomach. Placing a palm on the doorknob for balance, she wriggled each foot into red canvas espadrilles.

Logan stuck his head in the closet a moment later. She was having another contraction. "Aren't you cutting it a little close?"

"Not in the least," she informed him, straightening as the contraction passed. "This stage can last for hours." *I hope.*

The contractions were getting to be more painful than she'd been led to expect in Lamaze class. Not unbearable, by any means, just more painful than she'd expected them to be.

She brushed past him, heading for the bedside table.

"Now what are you doing?" He was about as near complete exasperation as he ever wanted to get.

"Calling my mother."

"You can call her from the hospital."

Catherine kept dialing. "There's plenty of time."

She reached her mother's answering machine. "Hi, Mom," she said to the tape. "It's me. I'm getting ready to head for the hospital. Bye." She pressed the plunger to get a dial tone and redialed.

"Who're you calling now?" Logan said the words softly, with all the patience he could muster.

"The kitchen at the main house," she said, listening to the phone ring at the other end. "Hi, Mom." It was obvious by her tone that she was talking to a real person this time. "It's time... Yes, I am... No, not too bad at all so far... About five minutes... Uh-huh... Uh-huh... I will, just as soon as he's born. I love you, too." She hung up the phone but didn't release it, leaning forward instead to brace herself. She took a deep breath through her nose and then let it out, slowly, through her mouth.

Logan stood stock-still for the full length of the sixty-second contraction, unconsciously breathing in time with his wife. "Are you ready to go *now*?" he asked when she straightened.

Catherine took an extra deep breath before she answered. That one had been just a little bit more intense than the last ones. Things really seemed to be progressing awfully fast. "Yes, I'm ready."

"Leave those alone, for God's sake," Logan said when she bent to pick up her dirt-smeared suitcases. "I'll get them."

"They need to be wiped off."

"I'll do it. You go on out and get in the car. Wait a minute," he said as she headed for the door. "You're not going
to take off without me again, are you?"

Catherine thought about it for a moment. It would serve
him right if she did but she wasn't in any condition to be
driving right now. "No, I won't drive off without you."

"Promise?"

She sighed deeply, just to let him know he was annoying
her. "I promise."

"All right," he agreed. "Go on and get in the car. I'll be
out in a minute."

He took the suitcases into the bathroom, gave them a few
quick swipes with the damp towel Catherine had used after
her shower, washed his hands and followed her out the car.

The suitcases he tossed into the back seat weren't quite as
clean as they could have been, and there was dirt smeared
across the front of his suit. It might have pleased Catherine
at any other time but she was too preoccupied to notice that,
for once, he was more untidy than she was. Another contraction was coming on.

"Those are coming less than five minutes apart," Logan
accused as he slid into the driver's seat.

"A little." She braced her hands on the dashboard, head
down, and began breathing slowly and evenly. "Oh, Lord!"
she gasped suddenly, digging her fingers into the soft leather
of the dashboard.

Logan gunned the engine to life.

The drive back into the city, with Catherine's contractions coming every four minutes or so, took even less time
than the drive out had taken. They picked up a cop about
five miles from the hospital but Logan ignored him.

"Oh, God. Stop the car. Stop the car," Catherine
moaned.

"Don't worry about the police. We'll be there in a minute."

"Stop the car!"

Logan pulled over.

Catherine pushed the door open and slid to her feet. Bending over from the waist, her hands braced on the top of the open door, she began to roll up on her toes in an odd little bouncing movement. It seemed to help the pain.

"Catherine, what are you doing?" Logan rushed around the long hood of the Jag. "Get back in the car." He tried to ease her back into her seat just as the policeman came even with the trunk of the Jag.

"Well, Mister," the cop began. "I hope you have a really good reason for— Holy cow, lady, you gonna have a baby right here?"

Logan shot him a look that could melt stone.

"You need an escort?" the cop said, hurrying back to his squad car as he spoke. "I'll give you an escort."

The contraction over, Catherine let herself be hustled back into the plush front seat of the Jag. It had hurt so much she wondered if they were going to make it to the hospital in time. Things were progressing so fast, even with the police car clearing the way with his red light and siren, her baby might end up being born in the front seat of a Jaguar.

Not a bad start, actually, Catherine thought, giggling to herself. There were undoubtedly worse places to be born. And think of the story she'd have to tell.

The thought was cut off, midgiggle, by another sharp contraction. She rocked forward with her arms clasped around her stomach, trying to approximate the bouncing movement that'd eased her last time. "Oh, it hurts. It hurts."

"I know, sweetheart," Logan soothed. "I know. Just hold on. We're almost there."

Catherine glared at him. "You *don't* know," she said, between deep breaths. "Don't say you know."

They screeched to a stop in front of the hospital. Logan shot out of the car, racing around the hood to open her door. The policeman was already out of his squad car, rushing to help.

"I can get out by myself, thank you very much," Catherine said, swatting at her husband's hands as he tried to help her out. "I don't need any help from a two-timing Lothario."

"From a what?" He grabbed her hands, pulling her to her feet. "What did you call me?"

"A two-timing Lothario," the cop said helpfully.

Logan looked at his wife. "What the hell does that mean?"

Catherine's water broke with a gush, turning the front of her denim jumper dark blue and running down her legs.

"Oh, my God." The policeman turned, heading toward the main door of the hospital at a run. "We need a doctor out here," he bellowed. "On the double. This woman's having a baby!"

Catherine looked down at the spreading stain on her denim jumper and the puddle between her splayed feet and started to cry.

Logan stooped, lifting her into his arms, and hurried toward the hospital entrance.

"Put me down!" *Oh, God!* Not only did she look a complete mess but now Logan was going to find out just how much weight she'd gained. She put her arms around his shoulders and hiccuped into his neck.

A nurse met them outside with a wheelchair. Logan ignored her, intent on getting Catherine inside himself.

"Hospital policy, sir," the nurse said, following him into the hospital with the wheelchair rolling along in front of her.

"Just put her down and we'll take it from here. She'll be fine."

"Dr. Kelson was supposed to meet us here," Logan said. "Dorothy Kelson. Is she here yet?"

"I'll have to check. Please, put your wife down. I'll have an aide wheel her up to maternity while you sign the forms."

"To hell with the forms." Logan's teeth were clenched with the effort to keep from bellowing like a madman. "Her contractions are less than five minutes apart, dammit!"

Catherine moaned, curling into the contraction so sharply that Logan was very nearly unbalanced. He let her feet slide down, holding her as she leaned against him. "Oh, God, it hurts!" she wailed, digging her newly strong nails into his arm through the fabric of his jacket and shirt.

"Just take it easy, honey," the nurse said. "Deep breaths. Take a big deep breath through the nose. That's it. Hold it for a second. Now let it out. Okay, again. That's it."

The contraction peaked and passed, leaving Catherine scared and trembling. *Was it supposed to happen this fast?* She sank into the wheelchair and wiped her eyes. "That one hurt so bad! Worse than the others."

"Your water just break?" the nurse asked, indicating the soaked front of Catherine's jumper.

"When I got out of the car."

The nurse nodded knowledgeably. "The contractions usually get more intense after the water breaks," she said, pushing the wheelchair toward the bank of elevators at the back of the building. "It's perfectly normal."

Logan trailed anxiously along behind them with another nurse right beside him, badgering him about the forms he had to sign.

"We've already filled out all the damn forms," Logan said through clenched teeth. "It's all in your computer. Fletcher. That's *F-L-E-T-C-H-E-R*. First name, Catherine, with a *C*. Now leave me alone and let me take care of my wife!" He stepped onto the elevator just before it closed.

Catherine had two intense contractions, one immediately after the other, on the way up. "Ohdearohdearohdear," she chanted on a rising inflection as the second one gripped her.

Logan crouched beside her. "Breathe, sweetheart. Like we learned in class, remember? Slow, deep breaths." He drew air in through his nose, blowing it out through his mouth to show her.

"Screw breathing," she said.

Logan laughed. He couldn't help it. What she'd said, and the way she'd said it, was so unlike the sweet, gentle Catherine he knew.

She glared at him as if he were a particularly ugly bug on a pin.

Logan stifled his laughter and stood.

The admitting nurse turned them over to a fourth-floor maternity nurse. "You'll be more comfortable in a few minutes now," she said to Catherine. "Marcia here will get you into a birthing room and give you a quick exam after you get into a gown. How does that sound, honey?"

Catherine gave her a wide, false smile. "Just hunky-dory, honey."

Logan smothered another laugh; Catherine was showing a side of herself he'd never seen before.

"How far apart are the pains?" asked Marcia as she took charge of Catherine's wheelchair.

"About four minutes. Maybe a little less," Logan answered.

"Mr. Fletcher hasn't signed the necessary papers," the admitting nurse said, stopping them before they headed down the hall.

"As I told you before," Logan said, "we've already filled out the paperwork."

"Yes, but you haven't signed the admitting forms."

Logan ran his hand through his hair. "Can't I sign the damn things later?"

"I want my suitcases," Catherine said, deciding the issue.

"You go on," the maternity-ward nurse advised him. "I'll get her examined and changed into a gown. By the time you get back she'll be all cleaned up and feeling much better."

"Like hell," Catherine muttered. She knew, instinctively, that it was going to get much worse before it got better.

"All right." Logan leaned down and kissed his wife on the cheek. "I'll hurry." He entered the elevator with the nurse from admissions.

The maternity-ward nurse began to wheel Catherine down the hall. "Well, now," she said, smiling. "Let's get you into a birthing room and see what we've got."

Nine

Catherine's suitcases and the keys to his Jag were waiting for Logan at the admissions desk. The policeman who'd provided them with an escort had taken care of it. In less than five minutes, Logan had signed the necessary forms and was on his way back up to the maternity ward.

Oh, God, he thought, running a hand through his hair as the elevator ascended, *this is it. This is really it!* He was about to become a father. A jumble of conflicting emotions—fear, joy, excitement—roiled around inside him, not completely unlike the ones he'd experienced when he first realized he was in love with his wife.

He stepped off the elevator. "Catherine Fletcher?" he said to the nurse behind the counter.

"Room 412. Down the hall to your left."

"Is Dr. Kelson here yet? Dr. Dorothy Kelson?"

"I believe she's with the patient."

Oh, God, it was happening without him! He took off at a jog.

From behind one of the closed doors in the wide, bright hallway, a woman screamed. It wasn't a scream of fear but of pain; a low wail that built in volume until it ended on an upward note of strain. Every hair on his body lifted.

Was it Catherine? he wondered frantically, checking door numbers as he went. The scream came again. *Not Catherine.* And not exactly a scream of pure pain, either. It was more like one of those shouts made by martial arts experts before they broke a brick in half, a verbal focusing of every available ounce of energy. Still, he hoped Catherine wasn't going to scream like that.

If Catherine screams like that I don't think I can stand it.

The door of room 412 was partially closed. Should he knock? Should he just barge right on in? He stood outside the door with a suitcase in each hand, part of him hoping he was in time to see his child born, part of him hoping it was all over and he wouldn't have to watch Catherine suffer anymore.

Coward, his better half sneered. He'd helped create the life she was laboring to bring into the world, the least he could do was offer his support while she did it.

He tucked Catherine's overnight case under his arm, freeing his right hand, and knocked. The maternity-ward nurse, Marcia, opened the door. The room was dim, except for the doctor's portable examining light, and quiet. No deep breathing. No moans. No screams.

"Come on in," Marcia said, reaching for the two small suitcases he held. "We were just finishing up."

"Finishing up? You mean the baby's already here?" He was glad, of course, for Catherine's sake, that it had gone so fast but disappointed—yes, definitely disappointed—he hadn't been there to share it with her.

"No, not the baby," the nurse said softly. "That'll be a while yet. Dr. Kelson's just finished examining your wife."

"She's dilating nicely," Dorothy Kelson said. "Working on seven centimeters already."

"Is that good?" Logan hurried over to his wife's bedside. "Should it happen so fast?"

"The faster, the better," Catherine said from the bed. "Oh, Lord, here comes another one." She rolled sideways, swinging her feet over the edge of the bed and grabbed for the nearest support—the doctor's arm—to pull herself to her feet. With her hands braced on the other woman's forearm, Catherine came up on her toes and made the same little bouncing movement as she had when she yelled at him to stop the car.

Logan looked over his wife's head at the doctor.

"She knows what feels best," Dr. Kelson said in answer to his silent question. She looked down at his dirty suit. "Have to change a tire on the way here?" she asked.

"No, I—"

Catherine looked up, her glare daring him to tell the doctor what she'd done with her suitcases.

"Something like that," Logan said.

"Well, you don't have to scrub but I think you'd better wash up. Marcia," she said to the nurse, "would you have somebody bring Mr. Fletcher a pair of scrub pants? You can use the bathroom," she said to Logan. She put her arm around Catherine's shoulders, helping her walk toward the window as the contraction eased. "I'll take care of your wife until you're ready to take over."

Logan retreated into the small bathroom. Taking off his soiled jacket, he unbuttoned his cuffs, rolled the sleeves back with a few quick gestures and reached for the faucet. He hesitated for a moment, listening to the murmur of feminine voices coming to him through the door. The doctor said something he couldn't hear, making Catherine laugh softly. It was a sputtering sound as if whatever the doctor had said had surprised her, ending in a gasp of pain as another contraction gripped her.

He turned the water on with a savage twist and reached for the soap. He was on his second rinse when the nurse knocked on the bathroom door.

"Got your pants," she said, handing them to him as he opened the door.

They were big and baggy, with a drawstring waist. He pulled them on over his trousers without closing the door, watching the doctor and his wife as they paced slowly between the window and the bed. She seemed calmer than she'd been when they first got to the hospital but more fragile, more... More what?

Scared, he thought. She looked scared and small and defenseless, like a little girl who didn't know what was going to happen next, only that it was going to hurt.

He resolved to put on a brave front, no matter how much he was trembling inside. The last thing Catherine needed right now was to feel the fear that was gripping him, even if it was all on her behalf. It could only make hers worse.

"Clean enough?" he asked, his eyes still on his wife as he held his hands out to the nurse for inspection.

"As a whistle," the nurse said.

He brushed by her with a nod, intent only on Catherine.

The doctor looked up as he approached. "She's doing fine. Everything's perfectly normal."

"Catherine?"

"I'm fine," she said, her eyes on the floor. "I just need to walk."

Dr. Kelson stepped back, letting Logan take her place beside his wife. "Keep one hand right here." She placed it on what used to be Catherine's waist. "It'll support her and you can feel the contraction when it starts."

Catherine let him take her weight against him. They walked silently.

"She'll probably want to lean on you and bounce when the contraction starts, but if she wants to crouch or get on all fours or lie down, let her. Okay?"

Logan nodded.

"I'm going to check on another patient. Someone who had a baby yesterday, so don't worry," she assured him when he frowned. "I won't be busy when your wife needs me. Marcia will be right outside the door. If you need her, just holler. She'll see that I get here in plenty of time."

He nodded again, his eyes on his wife's profile. Fine, pale strands of her silky hair were clinging to the damp skin of her cheek. He brushed them gently away, not even noticing when the doctor left.

They continued walking. Five steps to the window, turn, and five steps back, stopping approximately every three minutes for the contractions. Catherine never took her eyes off the floor. It took Logan a while to realize she was counting the floor tiles, over and over, as a way of focusing.

He thought of the glass hummingbird she'd packed for the purpose. Should he take the time to dig it out of her suitcase? No, he thought, she seemed to be doing just fine with the alternate method she'd chosen. To leave her side now and look for the glass bird might break her concentration. Things had progressed so quickly, they hadn't used any of the aids to natural childbirth. So much for "modern" medicine, Logan thought.

The nurse, Marcia, popped her head in once. "How're the contractions coming? Do you feel like you need to lie down yet?"

"Not yet," Catherine murmured.

"Well, it shouldn't be too much longer," Marcia said cheerfully.

Logan wondered how much longer was *too much longer*? He had no idea how long they'd been pacing. Twenty minutes? An hour? Two? However long it was, he didn't think Catherine could take much more. And, if she could, then he damn well couldn't.

He could feel each of her contractions begin under his hand. They tightened the muscles in the back of her waist, where his palm rested, undulating under his fingers toward the front of her body like a boa constrictor, coiling tighter and tighter, until they finally peaked at the top of the sixty-second cycle, and then gradually released her.

Each one seemed to be getting worse, leaving her more breathless, more exhausted, taking more out of her—and him.

He felt so damned useless! And so guilty. It was so unfair that she should have to go through all this for something they were both responsible for. *Someone,* he thought, *should have arranged things better.*

As time passed, Catherine seemed barely able to tolerate his touch. She allowed him to support her as she walked but that was all. When he tried to dab the moisture from her upper lip or brush back the fine, damp hairs at her temples, she swatted his hand away.

"Don't touch me!" she snarled at him. Her skin felt stretched and too tight, sensitive to the slightest touch. "I don't want you to touch me!"

Finally, she even refused his support. "This is all your fault," she accused, hanging on to the back of the only chair in the room as her contraction subsided. "You got me pregnant on purpose!"

Logan didn't have anything to say to that. He *had* gotten her pregnant on purpose. But it wasn't as if she hadn't known what he was doing—or participated most enthusiastically while he did it.

"And when I got too fat and ugly for you to want any-more, you went out and found yourself some—" a con-traction bit into her with savage intensity "—someone else." She gasped as it rolled through her.

"Someone else?" He reached out, wrapping his arm around her shoulders as she started to hunch over. "Who? Who said I didn't want you?" Didn't she know he wanted her with every breath he drew?

She accepted his support as the contraction tightened and peaked, panting for all she was worth, then pushed him away when it was over. "You didn't think I knew," she said wildly. "But I did and— Don't touch me!" She backed away a few steps and then suddenly hunched over again as another contraction hit her. It had been less than a minute since the last one. *"Oh, God, it hurts!"* The last word was a scream that brought Marcia at a run.

"I have to lie down," Catherine gasped disjointedly. "Lie . . . down. *Now.*"

Logan and the nurse were already lowering her to the bed. She drew her knees up. "Got to push," she panted.

"Take it slow and easy," Marcia warned. She pressed the call button as she spoke. "Just take it slow and easy and you'll be fine."

"OhGodohGodohGod," Catherine moaned, as the con-traction subsided and then built again almost immediately. There suddenly didn't seem to be any breathing space be-tween each one. "I can't do it, Logan." She grabbed his arm, nearly tumbling him onto the bed on top of her. "I can't do it. It hurts too much."

All the blood drained from Logan's face as he cradled his travailing wife in his arms. *"Where's the damned doctor?"*

"The damn doctor's right here," said Dorothy Kelson, hurrying into the room in answer to the nurse's summons.

With the synchronized teamwork of hundreds of births attended together, the two medical women sprang into action. Dr. Kelson washed her hands in the bathroom sink, thrust her hands into the surgical gloves Marcia held for her, and perched between Catherine's widespread thighs with the portable light right where she needed it.

"Okay, let's see what we've got," the doctor said, quickly but gently examining her patient. "Looks like we're just about ready."

Logan found himself kneeling behind his wife on the bed, supporting her upper body like a human armchair.

"I've got to push!" Catherine screamed.

"Do it easy," the doctor said. "Nice and easy. We don't want you to tear. That's it. You're doing good, Catherine. Everything's coming along perfectly. That's it. *Push.*"

She heaved herself up to almost a sitting position with Logan behind her, supporting her weight, offering her encouragement, and curled her hands under her thighs, pushing with all her might. There was nothing ladylike or delicate about the sound she made. It was pure, unadulterated female, struggling to give birth.

"Good, Catherine. Good. You're doing fine."

Catherine collapsed back against her husband, panting like an asthmatic, overheated pug.

"Okay, give me another one. Come on, *push.*"

She took a deep breath and heaved herself up again.

"That's it, I can see the top of his head! He's almost here. That's it. Push, Catherine!"

"I'm pushing, dammit!"

"You're doing great, sweetheart," Logan said in her ear. "Just great."

Catherine screamed as her baby's head slipped out of the birth canal.

Logan hugged her as tightly as he could, trying, in some small way, to share her pain.

"Here he is!" Dr. Kelson was as excited as if she'd never delivered a baby before. "Here he is!"

The nurse moved in, suctioning his tiny nose and mouth, wiping his sopping wet head with a warm towel. He opened his mouth and began to howl.

"I think we've got a ten, here, folks," Dorothy Kelson said with satisfaction, referring to the Apgar scale for rating a newborn's condition.

"Let me see." Catherine was reaching down to touch her baby. "Let me see. Oh, Logan, look." Tears were streaming down her face. "Look, he has dark hair, just like you."

"And your sweet little chin," Logan said softly, unaware of the tears sliding down his own cheeks.

They gazed down at their son with unutterable love filling their hearts. His little eyes were squeezed tight, his tiny face furiously red as he let them hear his displeasure.

Logan laughed softly, delightedly. It was the most beautiful sound he'd ever heard.

Catherine sighed. "He's so beautiful."

"Okay, quit admiring him for just a minute and give me one more push," Dr. Kelson said, delicately maneuvering the baby in preparation for releasing the shoulders. "One more big push. That's it. That's it."

Supported in her husband's arms, Catherine pushed. "Arrrgh!" she bellowed, giving it her last ounce of effort.

The shoulders came free, the rest of the body spurting out as if it were screaming down a water slide. Marcia deftly caught him in a warmed blanket, wrapping him to preserve precious body heat, and dabbed his face to remove the worst of the mess. "Try to get him to nurse," she said, placing the howling baby on his exhausted, exhilarated mother's chest.

He began rooting around immediately, his tiny rosebud mouth working as he searched for his mother's nipple.

"Definitely a ten," Dr. Kelson said as he found it and began to suck strongly.

"Oh, Logan, look," Catherine whispered, aglow with the light of instant, adoring, unconditional maternal love. "Just look at him.'' She stroked his damp curls with gentle wondering fingertips. ''Isn't he the most beautiful baby you've ever seen?''

''Beautiful,'' Logan said, gazing down at his wife's rapt face. ''Absolutely beautiful.'' He looked at his son. ''Welcome to the world, little Zacariah.''

The nurse had to nudge him twice to get his attention.

''Me?'' he said, staring down at the surgical scissors she held out to him.

She grinned at the shocked expression on his face and slapped them into his palm. ''Least you can do,'' she said. Saying a quick, silent prayer, Logan cut the umbilical cord.

Two hours later, Catherine awoke to the sound of soft, sporadic conversation that seemed to be coming from a long way off. She lay with her eyes closed for a moment, silently taking a physical inventory. She was still exhausted, of course, and as sore as if she'd run a marathon and then done a thousand sit-ups with a grown man sitting on her stomach. But she was clean and warm and dry. And, thankfully, she didn't have to endure the pinch of stitches when she moved her legs.

She hadn't required an episiotomy to avoid tearing during delivery. Despite the relatively short time she'd been in labor—two hours and twenty minutes from the time she arrived at the hospital—everything had stretched beautifully, accommodating the head and shoulders of her new son without a problem.

Her new son.

That first glimpse of him had been so... What was the word she wanted? Overwhelming? No, that wasn't enough. It had been an all-encompassing experience, involving all of her being. Her mind, her heart, her soul—every part of her had been consumed with the miracle of his birth.

Thinking of him made her breasts ache. She opened her eyes, knowing he'd be in a clear-sided hospital bassinet next to her bed. But he wasn't.

Logan sat in the chair next to her bed, almost within hand's reach if she cared to make the effort, totally engrossed in the bundle of pale blue, bunny-strewn blankets in his lap.

"You gave your mother a lot of trouble, did you know that, Zacariah?" he said softly. "Eight pounds and twelve ounces of trouble. It's a good thing you didn't wait any longer to put in an appearance."

An incredibly tiny hand, its fingers curled into a lax fist, appeared above the edge of the bundle.

Logan touched it wonderingly, brushing the pad of his index finger over the backs of his son's. "You're a fine, big boy, aren't you?"

The tiny fingers uncurled, grasping his index finger as if in answer.

"Strong, too." He pulled a little, very gently, but the baby didn't let go. "Look at that grip," Logan said proudly. "You've got the grip of an NFL player already, don't you?" He bent his head closer to the bundle in his lap. "Don't tell your mom—" he kissed the tiny fingers clasping his "—but I'm going to get you a football to go with all those non-sexist toys in your new room."

Catherine felt her heart turn over with a love so sharp and intense it almost hurt.

"And a dog," Logan said. "Every little boy should have his own dog. How about a collie? Or a Lab?"

The baby cooed softly, as if in agreement, and pressed a tiny foot to his father's stomach.

"A Lab it is, then." Logan kissed his son's foot. "Lab's are good."

He went on talking gently to his son, forging the beginnings of a strong, loving bond as Catherine lay there, watching silently with tears of love in her eyes.

"Oh, now, don't do that," Logan said a moment later as the baby started to fuss. "You'll wake up your mom, and that wouldn't be nice, would it? After all the trouble you put her through? She needs her sleep." He rewrapped the blanket in an approximation of the way he'd been taught in his "fathers only" class and slipped his hand under the baby's head, awkwardly lifting him to his shoulder. "Hush." He gently patted the baby's back, nearly covering the newborn's body with his hand. "Hush, now."

The ache in Catherine's breasts intensified at the newborn's cry. "Give him to me," she said.

Logan looked at her over the baby's head. "We didn't mean to wake you."

"I was awake." She pushed herself to a sitting position and held out her arms. "He wants his mommy." She knew because his mommy wanted him.

Very carefully, Logan stood and then bent over from the waist, lowering his son into his wife's waiting arms. As she took him, gingerly settling him into the crook of her arm, Logan arranged the pillows behind her.

"Stay here with us," she said as Logan started to sit down in the chair again. She patted the bed beside her. "Right here."

Logan looked longingly at the spot she indicated. "It won't bother you if I sit on the bed?"

"No, of course not."

It would be easier to nurse Zacariah this first time—somehow putting him to her breast just after his birth didn't count as the first time—with Logan beside her, looking down, instead of sitting in the chair where he could stare directly at her. Despite all they'd shared in the past six hours, she was still sensitive about the changes in her body since the last time he'd seen her naked. She wasn't taut and firm anymore; she was a woman who'd borne a child and it showed.

Nervously she unfastened the first few buttons down the front of her rose-sprigged eyelet nightgown as Logan settled down beside her. His right arm curled, quite naturally, over the pillows behind her so that she and the baby were sheltered in the curve of his arm. Pushing the material of her nightgown back just enough to bare her nipple, she put the baby to her breast.

He stopped fussing immediately, rooting around with his mouth open until he clamped on to his mother. She jumped at the sensation.

"Hurt?" Logan said, immediately concerned.

"No." She shifted the baby slightly, settling him more firmly against her. "I just wasn't expecting it."

As the baby began to suck more strongly, setting up a rhythm against her breast with his mouth and his tiny kneading fist, she felt it in her womb. Definite tuggings and pullings, like mild cramps. It startled her for a moment until she remembered the Lamaze teacher telling the class that nursing stimulated the uterus to contract to its natural size more quickly. This, then, must have been what she'd been talking about.

"He's a greedy little pig, isn't he?" Logan said softly. His voice was warm and full of amused pleasure.

"He's just hungry," Catherine said. "He had a hard day and he needs his nourishment. Don't you, darling?" she murmured, bending her head to kiss the baby's soft spot. "Not that he's really getting anything besides colostrum," she added, referring to the thin, nourishing fluid that precedes breast milk. "But he likes it." Then, while he continued to nurse, she folded his blanket back to look at him.

He was so tiny. But so perfect. Wonderingly, she measured his foot against her hand and found it was barely as long as her little finger. With a careful fingertip, she touched his rosy cheek and the curve of his ears and his little rounded knees.

"Look at his fingernails," she said to Logan, who'd made his own investigation while she slept. "They're so small! And his eyelashes. He even has eyelashes!"

It was only when he started, in that sudden way that babies have, his little arms and legs jerking suddenly, that Catherine covered him up again.

They sat silently for a few moments more, the picture of the perfect new parents, watching their newborn son nurse. Catherine relaxed, settling back so that her head rested against her husband's encircling arm. Logan lifted his left hand to stroke the soft wispy curls on the baby's head. Once, twice, a third time. The motion seemed to lull all three of them.

"Catherine?"

"Hmm-mmm?"

"About—" Logan swallowed. He didn't really want to bring it up now but he had to know. Had to set straight whatever needed setting straight. Catherine and the baby were too important to him not to. "About what you said."

"What I said about what?" Her voice was dreamy and content, like that of a woman on the verge of sleep.

"About the marriage not working."

Without moving a muscle, she came fully alert. "Did I say something about the marriage not working?"

"Yes, and you said I didn't want you, either. You accused me of finding someone else."

Oh, God, not now! I don't want to talk about it now. "Did I?" She tried to sound unconcerned. "I don't remember."

"But you said—"

"Oh, you know what the Lamaze teacher said about women in labor." She chuckled, fighting down the sudden nausea his words brought. "We say all kinds of things we don't mean."

The baby let go of her nipple and started to fuss. She jiggled him slightly, making soothing noises as she tried to direct him back to it.

"Did you?" Logan asked.

"Did I what?" she asked, as if she'd forgotten what they were talking about.

"Did you say things you didn't mean?"

"I must have," she said, "because I don't remember saying much of anything at all except 'it hurts.'"

Zacariah started to cry in earnest.

"Here it is, darling," Catherine crooned, still trying to get him to take her nipple. "See? It's right here."

The baby continued to cry, turning his head away from her breast.

Logan got to his feet, made nervous by the baby squalling for no reason he could see. Their conversation seemed suddenly unimportant in the face of the baby's furious tears. "What's wrong with him?"

"I don't know," Catherine said. She felt like crying herself until a thought occurred to her. "Maybe it's his diaper." She shifted him, folding back his blanket so she could check. The diaper was wet.

"Get me a clean one, would you please?" she said, putting the baby down beside her so she could unfasten the diaper tabs.

"Where are they?"

Catherine looked up at him. "Don't you know?"

He shook his head. "Should I call a nurse?"

Catherine nodded. "I guess you'd better."

The subject, they both thought with relief, *was closed.* At least for now.

Logan promised himself he would bring it up again later.

Ten

———

How long, Logan wondered, *did postpartum depression last?*

Not that Catherine was depressed, exactly. Any fool could see she was ecstatic about the baby; motherhood suited her even better than pregnancy had. But she was just— Hell, he didn't know what she was!

True to his promise to himself, he tried bringing up the matter of all the accusations she'd spouted at him during labor. More than once, in fact. But she always managed to brush it aside somehow. "A woman says all kinds of crazy things in labor, Logan," she said. Or, "Are you sure you heard me say that? I don't remember it." Or, "Please, Logan, I'd really rather not talk about it now. I'm very tired."

She was tired a lot of the time and prone to tears for no reason he could see. As moody as a teenage girl around him.

He'd thought he was prepared for that—he'd read enough about it that he should have been prepared—but he wasn't.

He'd handled it all wrong when he found her standing in front of the bedroom mirror three weeks after Zacariah's birth with half a dozen of her prematernity slacks scattered at her feet, crying in frustration because nothing fit right.

"Sweetheart, nobody expects you to fit back into your regular clothes yet," he'd said, trying to soothe her.

It was the wrong thing to say, apparently. She'd just cried harder and fled into the bathroom, slamming the door behind her to keep him out.

The two caftans he'd bought her a few days later had been all wrong, too. He'd thought she'd be pleased to have something besides her maternity clothes or his sweatshirts to wear until she was back into her old things again. She'd thanked him pleasantly enough but the look in her eyes made him feel like the hunter who'd just killed Bambi's mother.

The worst thing, though, the absolutely worst thing was the way she fussed at him to leave her alone when she was nursing the baby. He *loved* to watch her nurse the baby. It made him feel warm inside, and not, he admitted, only in the region of his heart. Certain other parts of his anatomy heated up when she bared her lush breasts to their child.

And then she'd look up and catch him staring at her and shoo him away.

Of course, he told himself, she *was* upset about her inability to provide the baby's only source of nourishment. Despite the lushness of her breasts, they didn't seem to provide enough milk to keep Zacariah satisfied and, as a result, she'd had to supplement the baby's diet with formula. Everybody—her doctor, the people at La Leche, her mother—assured her it wasn't her fault and didn't mean she was a terrible mother. Zacariah was *not* going to be traumatized because he had to drink a little formula now and then. Lots of women had trouble at first, they told her, and when she was more comfortable with the whole process, when she relaxed, her milk would come more easily.

The trouble was, she couldn't relax when Logan watched her. She said he made her nervous.

He'd thought—hoped—it might get better after his mother-in-law left. Fiona had been an almost daily guest, popping in and out at all hours of the day with another new something she'd bought for her "precious baby" but Irene had moved in with them. It was only supposed to be for the first few weeks but, somehow, it had stretched to five.

Not, of course, that she wasn't a big help to Catherine—Logan felt like an ingrate when he found himself wishing she'd disappear—but things just couldn't get back to normal with a third wheel around all the time.

And he desperately wanted things to get back to normal.

Because, until things were normal, he couldn't even begin to seduce his wife into loving him.

Catherine knew she was acting like an unreasonable, ungrateful bitch. But she couldn't seem to help it.

To begin with, she was just so tired all the time. And when she was tired she didn't seem to be able to control her emotions as well as she usually did. Especially emotions that zigzagged from giddy happiness to utter despair in the blink of an eye.

She knew it was wearing on Logan. That he was puzzled by her behavior. And she would have explained—if she could have thought of a good explanation.

Like the day he'd caught her crying because none of her pants fit. It was a stupid, selfish thing to be doing, crying because she hadn't got her figure back yet when the reason she'd lost it in the first place was the sweet bundle of joy in the nursery. No reasonable person would expect to be back in shape only three weeks after giving birth. Logan certainly didn't expect her to be her old streamlined self; he'd come right out and said so.

She'd wanted to hit him for mentioning it.

And when he'd gone out and bought her those caftans—those loose, roomy caftans meant to camouflage a less than desirable figure—she'd wanted to hide.

If that's the way he felt about her, how were they ever going to get back to their old prepregnancy relationship?

It hadn't been perfect by any means but at least they'd been sleeping together. And if they didn't begin sleeping together again soon, if she didn't have some way to hold him besides the baby, she was going to lose him to Deirdre Walsh.

Maybe after her mother left, when they were alone again, just her and Logan and the baby, things would change. They had to because they couldn't go on the way they were for very much longer.

Things didn't change. Irene had been gone for a week, Catherine had had her six-week checkup, and things hadn't changed even one tiny bit.

Logan was about at his wit's end. He'd expected something, some indication, some little sign that she was ready to resume a full marital relationship. He didn't expect anything overt, nothing along the lines of "Okay, let's do it" but he'd expected *something*.

After all, she didn't mean to keep him out of her bed, so to speak, for the rest of their married life.

Did she?

Catherine was about at her wit's end, too. Her mother had been gone for a week, she'd had her six-week checkup and been pronounced "fit as a fiddle" and Logan still hadn't approached her.

She'd expected something—a hello kiss that lasted a bit longer than usual, a caress in the night—something that said he wanted to resume lovemaking.

Unless, she thought uneasily, *he never intends to resume lovemaking.*

Maybe he was getting all his "needs" met by Deirdre. Maybe he still had no desire to make love to his wife, even now that she was getting her figure back. Maybe he'd decided he'd turn their marriage into one of mere convenience, staying with her—Catherine—for the baby's sake and keeping his real love on the side.

If that's what he thinks, Catherine thought furiously, *he has another think coming!*

Things finally came to a head seven weeks to the day after Zacariah's birth.

Logan called to let Catherine know he wouldn't be home for dinner that evening. "A potential new client Ned thinks we need to wine and dine a bit," he said. "I won't be much past ten o'clock."

After he'd hung up, Catherine did something she'd never done before. She called the Baileys' number to check up on Logan's story. She wasn't sure what she meant to say, she hadn't given herself a chance to think it through. When Ned answered she didn't say anything at all. She didn't need to. Simply hearing Ned's voice gave her all the answer she needed.

Logan had lied to her.

He wasn't with Ned and a "potential new client." He was with Deirdre.

Something in Catherine snapped. Quietly, calmly, without fanfare or hysterics, it snapped.

I can't live like this anymore.

And when Logan came home she'd tell him so.

* * *

He stopped and bought roses on the way home at the twenty-four-hour florist he'd found the last time he bought her flowers. Two dozen blush pink roses like the ones she'd carried on their wedding day. He was tired of waiting. He was going to tell her tonight. He'd wake her up and just come right out and tell her how he felt.

She could take it from there.

He pulled his Jag into the garage next to her Mercedes, ran his hand through his hair and picked up the roses.

It was now or never. He couldn't take this wanting and not having a minute longer. Not one minute longer.

She was sitting at the kitchen table, a cup of coffee in front of her, waiting for him.

It kind of threw his timing off.

"Hello, Logan," she said, eyeing the roses. *Another guilt offering.* If she'd had any doubts about where he'd really been tonight, the roses cleared them up.

"Catherine." He wasn't quite sure what to say; he hadn't planned on her being awake. "What are you doing up?"

"Waiting for you."

"You didn't have to do that." He came across the room, leaned down and kissed her cheek.

She barely acknowledged him.

"These are for you," he said uncertainly, laying the roses on the table in front of her. *Maybe now isn't such a good time for that showdown, after all,* he thought. He could always tell her how he felt tomorrow.

She barely glanced at the roses. "Please sit down, Logan," she said, fingering her coffee cup. "I'd like to talk to you about something."

Definitely not a good time. "Can't it wait until tomorrow? I'm really bushed."

I'll bet, she thought. "It will only take a minute, Logan. Please, sit down."

He sat down.

Ten seconds dragged by.

Twenty.

"Catherine?"

She took a deep breath. "I can't go on like this any longer, Logan," she said, staring into her coffee cup. "I want a divorce."

Logan's mouth dropped open.

"You can see Zacariah whenever you want," she said. "We'll even have joint custody. Whatever you want. All I ask is that he not learn to call Deirdre, Mommy."

Deirdre? Logan thought, totally at sea. *A divorce?*

"If you'll agree to that up-front, I won't make a fuss. I know how you hate a fuss."

"A fuss," he sputtered. Here he was, ready to lay his heart at her feet, and she was talking to him about divorce!

"California's no-fault divorce laws should make it fairly easy," she went on calmly, still not looking at him. "I'll have to ask you for support, though. At least, at first, until I can get another teaching job."

Logan got to his feet, leaned over the table, and put his hands flat on either side of the roses.

Catherine forced herself to return his look calmly.

"What in hell are you talking about?"

Catherine blinked. She knew that tone; it meant he was angry. *But why was he angry?* She was giving him what he was too kind to ask for on his own, wasn't she?

"Don't look at me with those wounded deer eyes. It won't work this time." He lifted one hand and grasped her chin. *"I want to know why you want a divorce,"* he bit out, enunciating each word very, very carefully.

"Well, I . . ."

"I'm waiting."

She couldn't lie when he looked at her like that. "I don't," she said in a small voice. "Not really."

"You don't?" He let go of her chin and straightened. "Well, then—" he ran a hand through his hair "—I don't understand. What's this all about?"

"You and . . . and Deirdre."

"Me and Deirdre?"

Catherine nodded.

"Me and Deirdre what?" he said. There was no "him and Deirdre." There never had been. Never would be. She wasn't even his type; she was too much like his mother.

"Oh, please, don't be kind," Catherine said. "I've had enough of your kindness to last me a lifetime." She stood and carried her coffee cup to the sink. "I know all about you and Deirdre, Logan." She turned around to see his face when she accused him. "I've seen you."

"You've seen us what?" What could she have seen when there was nothing *to* see?

"The two of you, together. In your office," she added when he seemed to be waiting for more.

"In my . . ." Light suddenly dawned. "In my office. Of course! *That's* why you ran out that day in such an all-fired hurry. It wasn't because you were in labor, at all. It was because you saw—*thought* you saw," he amended, "Deirdre in my arms."

"She *was* in your arms! I know what I saw. She was crying on your shoulder and saying she couldn't 'live like this anymore.' Well, I can't live like this anymore, either, Logan! I want a divorce! Do you hear me?" She knew she was getting hysterical—a perfect imitation of Fiona at her best, she thought—and fell silent, struggling for control. "I want a divorce," she said quietly.

Something in Logan snapped. Whatever it was that had been holding him together for the past six months, whatever it was that had enabled him to be patient and understanding and self-sacrificing toward the woman who'd been causing him unprecedented emotional pain and mental anguish just suddenly let go. Towering, unexpected anger rushed in and took its place.

How dare she, he thought furiously, *how dare she stand there and say she wanted a divorce!* after all he'd done for her, all he'd endured for her, all he'd put up with *from* her!

He'd turned himself inside out trying to please her, dammit! He'd gone out for tacos in the middle of the night because she'd craved them. He'd bought gift after gift in an effort to find one that pleased her. He'd taken a back seat all during her pregnancy instead of being the full partner he'd wanted to be to keep from upsetting her. He'd put up with her moods and her easy tears and her injured silences without a whimper of protest or blame. He'd jumped through hoops for her, dammit, flaming hoops, including the one that had put him in a sexual deep-freeze for the past six months.

And now, just like that, she had the gall to stand there and say she wanted a divorce because she thought he was having an affair with a television sexpot who wasn't even remotely his type!

He reached out and grabbed her by the shoulders. "Was that what all that crazy 'two-timing Lothario' business was about?" he roared, beside himself with righteous anger and hurt feelings. "And all that screaming about me finding someone else? You thought I was having an affair with Deirdre Walsh? *Deirdre Walsh?*" He repeated the name as if he couldn't believe it. "Are you *crazy*?"

Catherine's eyes got as big as saucers. In all the twenty-seven years she'd known him, she'd never, ever seen Logan lose his temper. It stunned her into speechlessness.

He shook her when she didn't say anything. "Is this the thanks I get?" he demanded. "Accusations and distrust?"

"Th-thanks?"

"Yes, thanks, dammit! Thanks!" He was acting like a mad beast, the way he'd always been afraid he would act in a situation like this, but he couldn't seem to help it. He was hurting and angry and so much in love that he'd lost all reason. "For being so damned patient all the time, for tiptoeing around you as if you were some—some high-strung *princess*—" he flung the word at her as if it were a curse "—who was carrying the heir to the throne. For pretending—"

"Oh, God!" Catherine tugged against his hands, trying to break out of his hold. "I don't want to hear this!" She couldn't bear to hear all about how he'd gone out of his way to be nice to her because he felt guilty about being in love with another woman.

Logan's hands tightened in an effort to still her struggles. "Well, you're damn well *going* to hear it."

"No!" She wrenched herself away from him. "No! I won't listen to you tell me about your affair with Deirdre!" She put her hands over her ears and squeezed her eyes shut. "I *refuse* to listen."

He grabbed her wrists, dragging her hands away from her ears. *"I'm not having an affair with Deirdre Walsh!"* he shouted in her face. "Do you hear me? I'm *not*."

Catherine stared up at him for a long, silent moment. "You're not?" she said softly. Hopefully.

"No." Disgusted with himself, with her, he let go of her wrists and turned away. "I'm not."

Catherine stared at his broad back, a frown creasing her forehead as she tried to make sense of what she'd just heard. Logan said he wasn't having an affair with Deirdre Walsh and Logan didn't lie. But . . .

"I saw you," she said to his back. "That day in your office before Zac was born. I saw you. You had your arms around her. You were telling her everything was going to be all right. And I . . . I . . ." Her voice trailed off. What else was there to say? She'd seen what she'd seen.

"So," he stood facing the kitchen sink as he spoke, unwilling to let her see the pain her lack of trust caused him—or the impotent anger that still boiled under the surface, "on the basis of that one incident, you decided I was having an affair."

"Well, I..." It made her sound so unreasonable, put that way. As if she'd violated some wifely code by daring to judge him, by not trusting his integrity over the evidence she'd seen with her own eyes.

"You didn't even have the courtesy to ask me what was going on," he said fiercely, still not looking at her. "You just convicted me, then and there."

"Well, I..." She wrung her hands. Something about his voice, or the way he stood, or the set of his wide shoulders, made her feel dreadfully guilty all of a sudden. He sounded almost hurt, like a little boy whose best friend had found someone else to be best friends with. *Had* she convicted an innocent man on the basis of one misconstrued incident?

No, she told herself. No. It hadn't been just that one incident. It had been—*was*—a lot of other things, too. Small things, maybe, but they added up. Catherine lifted her chin, refusing to let him make her feel guilty. "I *saw* you." That, at least, was irrefutable.

He turned, pinning her where she stood with an accusing stare. He could feel the simmering anger rising in him again at her stubborn insistence on his guilt, and it took every ounce of willpower he had to tamp it back down. He would *not* let love turn him into a besotted, hysterical fool! He leaned back deliberately, resting his hips on the kitchen counter, and folded his arms across his chest. "Maybe you should have played the voyeur a little longer, Catherine," he said quietly.

She eyed him warily. "What do you mean?"

"You might have found out the truth."

"Which is?"

"The man Deirdre is having an affair with isn't me, it's Barnaby Webb."

"Barnaby?" Her eyes widened. Deirdre and Barnaby? The sexpot and the terminally shy accountant? How stupid did he think she was? "I don't believe it!"

He shrugged as if it didn't matter to him one way or the other whether or not she believed him. Except that it did. Too much.

"But...but she's not even his type!" Catherine sputtered.

"Maybe not. But the fact is, they *are* having an affair," he said, wondering why the hell he was even bothering to explain. Catherine was his wife; she should have trusted him without explanations. "She'd told him to 'fish or cut bait' and he's been having a hard time making up his mind. She was crying about him that day."

"On your shoulder?"

Logan shrugged again. "She seems to have cast me in the role of confidant."

Catherine eyed him for a long, considering moment, wondering if she could believe him.

He stared back, silently daring her not to.

She wanted to believe him. Oh, how she wanted to believe! But... "What about tonight?" she asked. "Was she crying on your shoulder tonight, too?"

"I was out with a client tonight."

"I called Ned's house, Logan. He was home."

"So?"

"So you said 'a potential new client Ned thinks we need to wine and dine.'"

"Ned does think we need to wine and dine him." He spoke quietly and very precisely, clear evidence to anyone who knew him that he was still very angry, despite his casual pose against the kitchen counter. Was she going to cross-examine everything he said? "So I was doing it."

"Without Ned?" Did he think she didn't know wining and dining clients was Ned's area of expertise and responsibility?

"Ned was otherwise engaged this evening. That's why I was doing it. Would you like me to get a signed affidavit from him?" he added when she didn't say anything.

"No . . . No, I believe you." She couldn't not believe him when he was standing there, staring at her with that look of righteous indignation on his face. But it didn't change anything, not really. Maybe he wasn't in love with Deirdre Walsh but he wasn't in love with his wife, either. "But I still want a divorce," she said sadly.

Logan could actually feel himself losing control again. That word—*divorce*—pushed him right over the edge. He couldn't think clearly when she said that word. He shoved away from the counter and came toward her with his hands out. "Why, Catherine?" he said as his fingers curled around her upper arms. "Why?"

"Because I . . ." What could she tell him? What could she say that wouldn't sound self-indulgent and whiny? Because I'm not the center of your universe? Because you don't love me to distraction? Because—

"Tell me why, Catherine," he said, shaking her.

"Logan, stop it. You're hurting me."

He let her go as if she were on fire. "Oh, God, I'm sorry." He ran his hands through his hair and then down over his face. Even the most idiotic and passionate of his mother's lovers had never resorted to physical violence, although, he recalled as the remembered sound of shattering porcelain echoed through his mind, Fiona had. And more than once. Maybe it was in his blood. Maybe he was doomed to act like a madman when he fell in love. Maybe he'd been right all along and it was better *not* to be in love. He rubbed his eyes with the heels of his hands, fighting the feeling of utter despair that washed over him at the thought.

"Logan?" Catherine's voice, soft and hesitant, called to him. He lowered his hands to see her standing there, staring at him with wide, unbelieving eyes.

He took a deep, shaky breath. "I'm sorry, Catherine. Are you all right?"

She nodded, unable to speak past the lump in her throat. Tears gathered, shimmering in her eyes.

Logan felt like the lowest kind of heel. "Oh, God, Catherine. Don't cry," he said, automatically reaching out to comfort her.

She shook her head and backed away without thinking.

His hands dropped. "You don't have to be afraid of me, I'm not going to hurt you again."

"No, it's not that. I—" She extended her hand toward him to show that she wasn't afraid, but he'd already turned away. She brought the hand to her mouth and pressed her fingers to her trembling lips.

She'd hurt him badly. How could she not have realized how badly he'd be hurt by her accusations and distrust?

What was the matter with her?

This was Logan. Her best friend. Her husband. The father of her child. The man she'd known and loved for so many years. And in all the years she'd known him, he'd never lied to her. Not once. Not even a little white lie. In fact, he'd never done even one dishonorable thing in his entire life. So what made her think, even for a moment, that he'd cheated on her with Deirdre? Logan would no more have done that than he would have lied about it if he had! She should have known that if Logan had fallen in love with Deirdre—or with any woman—he'd have come right out and said so, not gone sneaking around behind his wife's back.

I must be crazy! she thought, knowing that, in a sense, it was true. She was crazy in love. Crazy with jealousy. Just plain crazy.

There was only way she could make it up to him. Only one way to make him understand why she'd acted the way she had. Only one way to take away some of the awful hurt she'd cause. "Logan, I—"

"I won't fight you on the divorce," he interrupted, afraid to hear what else she had to say. He couldn't take any more accusations, nor a litany of his faults as a husband. He didn't want a long, drawn out postmortem on his failed marriage. He just wanted... *Catherine*, he thought. Even now, after everything she'd said, he just wanted Catherine. Talk about a fool in love! "I'll get my things out of the house tonight."

"Oh, no!" It was an anguished cry, straight from the heart. "Oh, Logan, no."

He turned to look at her. "Then what?" he said sadly. "What is it you want from me?"

"I want... I want you to—" No, that was wrong. She couldn't expect him to do anything. She had to be the one to do it. She had to be the one to put her heart on the line. She should have done it when he asked her to marry him. It would have saved them both a lot of heartache.

She clasped her hands together and stared down at the floor. "I love you, Logan," she said quietly. "I've loved you since I was fifteen. I loved you when I married you and when I slept with you and when I had your baby. I don't want a divorce. I've never wanted a divorce, not really. What I really want from you, what I've *always* wanted from you is—" tears clogged her throat at the thought that she'd probably never have what she wanted most "—is for you to love me, too."

She looked up quickly, just long enough to see Logan's expression change. He was staring at her as if she'd lost her mind—or he'd lost his.

"I know it's probably not what you want to hear," Catherine said when he didn't speak. "Oh, who am I trying to kid? I *know* it's not what you want to hear. But I had to say it, Logan. I couldn't keep it inside any longer.''

Ten long seconds ticked by in complete silence.

"*Say* something, Logan," Catherine burst out. "Say anything. Say you hate me, or that you—"

"You love me?" he said, as if he couldn't quite believe what he'd heard.

"Yes."

There was another seemingly endless second or two of silence as he digested that.

"And you loved me when you married me?"

Catherine nodded. "I wouldn't have married you if I hadn't.''

Logan frowned at her as he tried to puzzle that out.

Oh, God, she thought, *here it comes. Here's where he breaks what's left of my heart into a million tiny pieces.*

"And you've *always* loved me?" he persisted, wanting to make absolutely sure he understood her. Because if she loved him, if she'd always loved him, then why all the accusations and the tears and the pulling away from him in bed? "Since you were fifteen, you've loved me?"

"Yes, Logan."

"You're sure?"

"*Yes*, Logan." She closed her eyes, still fighting tears. This was the end of it, for sure. If she hadn't driven him away before with her moods and her suspicions and her appalling lack of trust, she'd done it now, with her bald-faced declaration of love.

He reached out for the third time that night and took her shoulders into his hands. "Then what in *hell* has all this been about?" he demanded. He didn't shout or even raise his voice above a normal speaking level but Catherine was left in no doubt as to the depth of his anger. "Why have I been pushed away, can you tell me that? Why have I been treated like some stranger you feel obligated to be polite to, hmm?'' He drew her up until she was practically standing on tiptoe. "And why, if you love me as you say you do, have you acted as if I have some deadly communicable disease every time I try to touch you?"

"Because I—" She swallowed in an effort to clear the lump in her throat. "Because I was afraid I'd drive you away if you knew how I really felt," she said, determined to make a clean breast of it now that she'd started. "I know how you feel about love. I know you don't believe in it but . . . but you're always so kind to me, anyway. I couldn't bear for you to be any more kind to me than you already were."

"*Kind?* You thought I was being *kind*?"

"You've always been so conscientious in your attentions to me," she explained. "Always so careful to say thank-you. Always making sure I knew my efforts were appreciated and—" she swallowed again "—and always so . . . so polite in bed that I—"

"*Polite!*" Was the woman crazy? He'd been wooing her with everything he had, twisting himself in knots in an effort to make her respond wholeheartedly, and she'd thought he was being *polite*?

"—and always so careful not to . . . not to . . ."

"Not to what?"

Two tears finally escaped her control and trickled down her cheeks. He wasn't going to leave her even a shred of pride. Well, fine, maybe she didn't deserve the solace of pride.

It was all he could do not to take her in his arms and kiss away her tears. But he held back, wanting everything absolutely clear first, refusing to live any longer with half-truths and evasions and misunderstandings between them. He might be in love, dammit, but he was through with acting like an idiot because of it. "I was always so careful not to what, Catherine?"

"Not to hurt my feelings. But—" she sniffed "—but they were hurt, anyway, because I knew you didn't want me and that's when I—"

"Wait a minute, here. You thought I didn't want you?" He slid his arms around her then, because he couldn't do anything else. Because he couldn't bear for her to think for even one more minute that he didn't want her. Not want her? How could he not want her when every cell in his body ached for her?

"You mean you did want me?" she said into his shirt-front.

"Oh, Catherine. Catherine." How could they have been at cross-purposes for so long? How could they—two sane, seemingly rational people—have both felt this way and yet not shown it to each other? He shifted his hands, gently cupping her cheeks as he lifted her face to his. "I want you with every breath I take," he said, staring down into her tear-bright eyes.

"You do?" she whispered.

"I do," he said solemnly.

"But I don't understand. When? Why? I mean, you didn't seem to want to...well, and you didn't even touch me after I started to show and I...I was afraid that..."

"What were you afraid of?" He brushed at her tear-streaked cheeks with his thumbs. "Tell me," he insisted. "Tell me now and then we'll put it all behind us."

"I was afraid you were turned off by my body," she said, finally giving him the gift of complete trust. "I got so huge and my ankles were all swollen and my breasts were all—"

"Your breasts were—*are*—beautiful," he said, stopping her with a fingertip over her lips. "Your breasts and your belly and even your swollen ankles. I loved looking at them—at you—even if I couldn't touch you. God, you don't know how many times I wanted to just reach over and put my hand on your belly or lay my head on your breasts and know I'd be welcome. Even if I couldn't make love to you, I just wanted to hold you. But I didn't think you'd let me."

"I wanted it, too," Catherine said fiercely. God, how she'd wanted it! "But I was afraid." She put her hands on her husband's chest and looked up at him with her whole heart in her eyes. "And I'm still afraid, Logan, because I still don't know. You haven't said and I can't—"

"I love you, Catherine," he said, astounded to find that it wasn't so hard to say, after all. It was so easy, in fact, that he said it again. "I love you."

"Oh, Logan." Her arms slipped up around his neck as he moved to cradle her close. "Oh, Logan."

Their lips met in a searing kiss—their first as true lovers. Their tongues touched and tasted each other. Their breaths mingled, moist and sweet with passion. Their lips touched and parted, then touched again as they tried new angles, new pressures, new approaches.

How long they stood there in the kitchen, reveling in their newfound love for each other, exchanging heated, soul-deep kisses and softly whispered lovers' promises, neither of them knew. But after a while, just kissing wasn't nearly enough. Not for either of them.

"I've wanted to touch you so badly for such a long time," Logan said against her mouth. "So badly. Here." He cupped her breast, cradling the lush, inviting fullness in his palm.

Catherine moaned.

"And here." He brushed his thumb over her enlarged nipple.

Catherine gasped.

"Did that hurt? Did I hurt you?"

"No. Oh, no." She took his hand and carried it back to her breast. "I've wanted your hands on me for months. Just like that. Oh, yes," she cried as he rolled her nipple between his thumb and finger. "Just like that," she sighed, letting her head drop back as he nuzzled his way down her throat. She straightened abruptly. "Oh, no."

He drew back to look down at her. "What is it?"

She blushed slightly and plucked at the front of her blouse. There was a small damp spot over her nipple. "I'm leaking milk. Not much, I don't think. I nursed Zac just before you came home."

"Milk? Really?" Logan was entranced. "I want to see." He began unfastening the small white buttons on the front of her blouse.

"Logan," she murmured, trying to catch his hand. It was so glaringly light in the kitchen. And she was still so unsure about his reaction to her changed body. "Logan, I—"

He evaded her hand, managing to open her blouse far enough to expose her lace-edged maternity bra. Eagerly he searched out the hooks that would release it.

"Logan, wait." She caught his hand, stilling it. "Wait a minute, please."

He stopped. "What is it?"

"It's not the same body you remember, Logan," she said, hoping she didn't look as red as she felt. "I'm not as firm and slim as I used to be."

"Catherine, I love you," he said, wondering how she could still doubt it. "I love our son. How could I not love the body that gave me that son?"

Without a word, she dropped her hand from his.

Slowly he unfastened the hook on her bra and peeled the cups back, one at a time. Her breasts—large, round, maternal, incredibly sexy—lay bare to his gaze. "Beautiful," he breathed.

"The nipples are huge," Catherine felt obligated to point out. It took all the willpower she possessed not to look down to see if they were leaking milk.

"Luscious." He ducked his head and took one deep rose nipple into his mouth. Very gently, he flicked it with his tongue.

Catherine whimpered with pleasure.

"They're more sensitive," he said, moving his head to taste her other nipple. "Tastier, too," he added, licking off the bead of milk that appeared in answer to his caress.

Catherine blushed with embarrassed delight.

"You did that the night I asked you to marry me."

"Did what?"

"Blushed. I forget why. But I wondered then if the color started at your breasts." He grinned at her. "It does," he said, bending his head to lavish his undivided attention on her breasts.

Catherine put her hands in his hair, holding him lightly, loving the feel of his mouth on her after so many months without him.

"This is going to add a whole new element to our love-making," he murmured when another drop of milk pearled on the very tip of her nipple.

"Do you mind?"

"No." He straightened to look at her. "Do you?"

Catherine shook her head. "Not anymore." She tightened her hands in his hair and pulled his head down to hers. "Make love to me, Logan. Please. I need you so much."

He took her mouth with his, reaching around her to cup his hands over the curve of her buttocks. Slowly, languidly, drawing out every exquisite sensation, he held her close and pressed himself against her while his tongue set up an insistent rhythm in her mouth. The air between them became moist and hot, filled with the ragged sighs and moans of unfulfilled passion.

He tore his mouth away from hers. "Jump up," he ordered, urging her with his hands on her bottom.

She complied eagerly, lifting her legs to wrap them around his waist. He carried her out of the kitchen and down the hall to their bedroom, kissing her all the way.

He dropped backward on the bed—the bed they'd slept in separately together for the past six months—taking their combined weight as they fell. His mouth was on her breast before they'd rolled completely over. He reached for the zipper of her pale blue slacks.

"I don't care if you're not as firm as some twenty-five-year-old starlet," he murmured as he pulled the zipper down. "I don't love some starlet. I love you." He slipped his hand inside her slacks and burrowed under the edge of the silky briefs beneath them. Delicately, very delicately and gently, he touched her.

She was hot and wet, more than ready for his touch.

His breath hissed out between clenched teeth. "Oh, Lord, Catherine, I've missed you!" Her back arched off the bed as he carefully slipped a finger inside her. "Missed this."

"Yes," she murmured, clinging to him. "Oh, yes." Her teeth sank into the white cotton fabric covering his shoulder. Frantically she kicked out of her slacks and panties and then lifted one leg, trying to swing it over his hip to bring him closer. "Oh, please."

"Please what? This?" He pressed her back down on the bed and rotated his hand against her mound. "Or this?" He began stroking her with a soft rhythm that threatened to drive her out of her mind. "I think that's it. Ah, yes, that's it." His voice was rich with masculine satisfaction as he watched her come apart in his arms. There was no reservation in her now, no holding back. She was his, totally.

"Oh, Logan. LoganLoganLogan*Logan!*" She stiffened, nearly screaming the last repetition of his name, and then fell back, panting and limp against the bed.

"You're sexier now," Logan said when she opened her eyes to focus on his face. "Your breasts." He passed a hand over each one in turn. "Your belly." He skimmed his palm over the curve of her stomach. It was still a bit swollen from the ordeal of her pregnancy, but even more beautiful to him because of that. "This," he said, cupping her between her thighs. "Do you know why you're sexier?"

"No." Her eyes were glued to his face, watching him as he watched his hand caress her. "Why?"

"Because it's the body of a real woman. A woman who's loved. Who's given birth. Who's nourished new life." He pulled her up over his recumbent form so that she straddled his hips. "Nourish me, Catherine," he whispered raggedly. "Love me." He put his hands on her arms to pull her down, his head lifting as he reached to take her breast into his mouth.

But Catherine had other ideas. It was her turn to show him how much, how very much, she loved him. Putting out a hand to stop him, she sat up and shrugged out of her blouse and bra, tossing them on the floor. Uncertainty gripped her for a moment, but only a moment. If Logan loved her body—and she believed him when he said he did— then she could do no less herself. Bravely she arched her back and thrust out her breasts, proudly displaying herself for his enjoyment. And, she found, for her own. Seeing the pleasure in his eyes as he looked at her, gave the pleasure back tenfold.

Then, more determined than ever to show him just how much she loved him and needed him and wanted him, she reached down and began unfastening the buttons on his shirt. She pulled the tails out of the front of his trousers, spread the shirt open and put her hands, palms down, fingers spread wide, on the flat plane of his stomach. Slowly, very slowly, she ran her hands up over his stomach and his rib cage and into the crisp black pelt of hair that covered the hard curves of his pectorals.

"I love your chest." She kneaded her fingers against him like a cat. "It's so hard and firm and it feels so good against my hands." She skimmed her hands along its width, up over his shoulders under the edges of the shirt, and then down again. "It's so broad and sheltering."

"Yeah?" He sounded a little embarrassed but she noticed he didn't tell her to stop.

"Umm-hmm. It's a chest you can depend on. A man with a chest like this could never do anything sneaky or dishonorable. A woman can trust a man with a chest like this." She bent down so that she was pressed against him from belly to breastbone, with her cheek resting on his shoulder and her face in the curve of his neck. "I love the way you feel against me," she said, nuzzling him with her nose. "The way your chest hairs tickle my nipples."

He murmured approvingly and ran his hand down the long curve of her spine, stroking her like a cat. She arched into his caress.

"I love the way you touch me, too." She sat up. "I love everything about you, Logan. Every last, little thing."

"Little?" he said, teasing her while he still could. He had an idea that, at any moment, she was going to drive him way beyond any ability to tease.

She rotated her pelvis against him, smiling when he stopped grinning and sucked in his breath. "And all the not so little things, too," she said and then moved against him again for good measure. It was one move too many.

Logan surged upward, wrapping his arms around her as he rolled her beneath him. "Playtime's over," he said, grinding into her as she locked her legs around his still-clothed hips. "I want you."

It took her a moment to catch her breath. "I want you, too." Lord, how she wanted him! "But let's get this off, first, okay?" She tugged at the shirt he still wore, helping him out of it as he freed first one arm, then the other. "And these," she said, slipping her fingertips under the waistband at the small of his back in an effort to push his slacks off.

"Wait." His voice was ragged. "Wait. I have to unzip them first."

She felt him lift off her slightly and then his hand came between them and the zipper rasped down. Catherine's fingertips touched the cleft of his buttocks. "Oh, Logan." She reached farther down, cupping her hands to pull him closer. "Oh, Logan. Oh—" She felt him slip inside, slowly, oh so slowly and carefully, as he tested her body's ability to accommodate him. *"Logan,"* she sighed, closing her eyes to relish the hard, hot feel of him after six long months of thinking he'd never make love to her again.

"Are you okay?" he asked raggedly. The strain of holding back, now that he was where he finally wanted to be, was nearly killing him. "Is it all right?"

"Oh, it's more than all right," she purred. "It's *wonderful!*" Her hands clenched on his buttocks, urging him to move.

He moved carefully at first, and then harder and faster as it became apparent her body was completely healed and there was only pleasure to be had from their coming together. His release was exuberant, a joyous culmination of all his dreams of what loving Catherine should be like.

"I love you, Logan," she murmured. "I love you so much."

When it was over, when they'd scaled the summit of physical passion and come sliding down the other side, there wasn't a single tear in sight.

They drifted in the delicious aftermath, replete and satisfied and renewed in each other's arms, talking about their wedding and their son and the moment they'd each first known they were in love with the other. And then, finally, he asked her about her first husband.

"If you've been in love with me since you were fifteen, then why'd you marry Kyle?" he asked, stroking her back as she lay sprawled half over him.

She stiffened slightly. "Oh, dear."

Logan was instantly apprehensive. "What?"

She came up on her elbow to look down at him. "Will you promise not to think I'm the biggest, most insensitive idiot alive if I tell you?" She was smiling slightly as she waited for his answer but he could see that she was serious.

"Tell me what?" he asked suspiciously, wondering what kind of bombshell she was going to drop on him now.

"Well-l-l . . ." She plucked at the hair on his chest. "It's not going to put me in a very good light," she warned.

He covered her restless hand with his, stilling it. "Tell me, anyway."

Catherine took a deep breath and said what she never thought she'd have to admit to anyone. "I only married him because he reminded me of you."

"You *what?*"

She hung her head. "Because he reminded me of you."

Logan didn't know whether to be amused or annoyed. He settled for being relieved. "Why?"

"Because, as I've already told you, I've been in love with you since I was fifteen years old. Crazily, desperately, hopelessly in love with you."

"So you married another man," Logan snorted. "That makes a lot of sense."

"It did at the time. You weren't interested in marrying me then. Or anyone else for that matter. And I didn't think you'd ever be. So I married Kyle."

"You could have asked me how I felt," Logan said, a touch huffily.

Catherine smiled at that. "And just what would you have said?"

"I'd've said . . . well, I'd've said . . ."

"Exactly."

"Well, it's still the craziest reason I've ever heard for marrying somebody."

"No crazier than marrying someone because she's your best friend."

His smile was smug and self-congratulatory. "It worked out, didn't it?"

"It worked out perfectly," she said, and leaned down to kiss him.

Epilogue

June, two years later

Put me down, you crazy man," Catherine said, laughing as her husband picked her up to carry her into the hotel suite. It was their third anniversary and Logan had "kidnapped" her for the weekend for a second honeymoon.

He'd made arrangements with Fiona and Irene to take care of Zacariah. A sturdy toddler now, he was probably running them ragged and making them love it; he had his father's roguish smile and his mother's sweet nature.

They'd driven down to San Diego in what Catherine would have sworn was the same white limo they'd ridden in on their first honeymoon, to the same hotel, to the very same room where they'd spent their wedding night. Everything, in fact, was the same. The room, the view, the green glass bottle in the silver ice bucket, the tray of fruit set out on the little round table in front of the window, even, she thought, the bellman who brought up their luggage.

Only they were different.

Because they were in love and it showed.

"Are you going to put me down or not?" she demanded of her husband.

"Not," Logan said, nuzzling her throat.

She laughed and nuzzled him back, completely ignoring the sidelong peeks the bellman was sending their way when he thought they weren't looking.

"He thinks you're crazy," Catherine whispered in her husband's ear.

"I am. About you." He set her on her feet and dug into his pocket for a couple of folded bills. "That'll be all, thanks," he said to the bellman before he could even begin to tell them about the amenities of the suite.

"Well, Mrs. Fletcher," he said when the bellman had gone, "would you care to slip into something more—" he wriggled his eyebrows suggestively "—comfortable before dinner arrives?"

"I think I just might at that," Catherine said, kissing him lingeringly before she picked up her overnight case and disappeared into the bathroom. "Don't go 'way."

Logan grinned at her. "Not a chance, lady."

Room service arrived while she was brushing her hair.

"Catherine, sweetheart." Logan tapped softly on the bathroom door. "Dinner's here."

"Be right out," she said, eyeing herself in the mirror. Her hair was a bit longer now, just past her shoulders, but still worn in a simple, straightforward style. Her nightgown was black silk, her peignoir chiffon. She'd searched nearly every lingerie shop and maternity boutique in L.A. to find it. She smoothed a loving hand over the prominent swell of her stomach. She was five months pregnant with twins according to Dr. Kelson, although she wasn't able to positively assure them of the sex this time.

·

It was really amazing, she thought, how different she felt this time around. Not about the baby, of course, but about herself. She didn't feel any less attractive or any less feminine because she was pregnant. That's what being secure in her husband's love did for a woman. Because he thought she was beautiful, she was.

"Catherine, it's getting cold."

She smiled at her image and opened the bathroom door.

The room was dim, lit only by the candles on the table and the amber-shaded glass lamp by the bed. Logan stood in profile to her, wearing the extravagant red velvet robe with the satin lapels she'd bought him on his last birthday.

"Makes me look like someone in an old Charles Boyer movie," he'd groused at the time. But he wore it to please her.

It looked magnificent on him, she thought as she stood there in the bathroom door, watching him pour sparkling cider into the two fluted, crystal glasses on the table. Red was definitely his color.

He looked up as if feeling her stare, smiling when he saw her. She was more beautiful than ever—her face shining with that special glow pregnancy gave her, her eyes alight with love, her lush breasts and protruding belly proudly, beautifully displayed to him through slinky black silk and airy chiffon that floated around her pale loveliness like a seductive cloud.

The rush of love and tenderness he felt every time he looked at her had ceased to surprise or upset him a long time ago. There was nothing upsetting about loving Catherine, nothing anxiety-producing or unreasonable. He'd learned that Fiona's way of loving was only one way; Catherine had shown him another, better way, no less intense for all its gentleness. She'd shown him that loving someone—passionately, romantically, completely—didn't have to turn a person into a raving lunatic.

As far as Logan was concerned, *not* loving Catherine would be insane.

"Mrs. Fletcher, I presume?" he said, holding out his hands to her.

She glided across the room to him. "Mr. Fletcher," she said softly, extending her own.

He caught her fingers in his and lifted them, one at a time, to his lips. "Have I told you today how beautiful you are?" he asked, kissing first one hand, then the other. "And how much I love you?"

"Yes," she said. "But you can tell me again."

He turned her hand over and pressed his lips to her palm. "You're beautiful." And then her other palm. "And I love you to distraction."

"I love you, too," she murmured.

"Shall we eat?" he said, letting go of her hands to pull out her chair.

After making sure she was perfectly comfortable, he went around the candlelit table and sat down across from her. "To love and marriage," he said, lifting his glass in a toast.

"To love," Catherine echoed softly, touching her glass to the rim of his, "and marriage. The very best kind of marriage," she added.

Logan lifted an eyebrow.

"One between friends," she said with a smile.

*   *   *   *   *

Silhouette Desire

COMING NEXT MONTH

ANOTHER WHIRLWIND COURTSHIP
Barbara Boswell

Four years ago Chelsea Kincaid had walked away from domineering Cole Tremaine, and he'd never forgotten it — or forgiven her! Now Chelsea had jilted the President's son and needed somewhere to hide. Cole would help, but at a price!

THE HEART MENDER
Kathleen Creighton

Love was the last thing brokenhearted Jenna McBride thought she needed. But when she met a dangerous-looking biker called Reno she was mesmerized. She thought she would have a fling, but how do you control your heart?

FREE TO DREAM
Janet Franklin

An idle month in the Rockies would feel like an eternity to efficient Andrea MacLarson. Then broad-shouldered drifter Bart Collins entered her life, and every minute with him became time well spent!

Silhouette Desire

COMING NEXT MONTH

JADE'S PASSION
Laura Taylor

Jade Howell had struggled to make her dream of a center for homeless children become a reality. There wasn't room in her life for a man — especially Reed Townsend, who had a secret that could tear them apart.

MAGGIE'S MAN
Jackie Merritt

Sloan Prescott had more on his mind than grazing rights when he thought of Maggie Holloway. He meant to keep his sheep on her land, but more importantly he meant to keep his boots under her bed — for good.

TWICE IN A BLUE MOON
Dixie Browning

Years before, January's *Man of the Month* Tucker Owen, had been the town's 'bad boy' — and loving Hope Outlaw, the preacher's daughter, had been an impossible dream. But that was then ...

Four Silhouette Desires absolutely free!

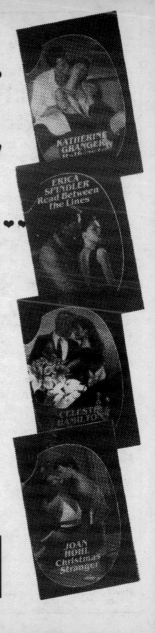

♥♥♥♥♥♥♥♥♥♥♥♥♥♥♥♥♥♥♥♥♥♥♥♥♥

P rovocative, highly sensual love stories designed for the sophisticated reader. The enticing plots provide a distinctive mix of exciting romantic encounters and unpredictable reactions.

Now you can enjoy four Silhouette Desire romances as a free gift from Silhouette plus the chance to have 6 more delivered to your door every single month.

Turn the page for details of how to apply, and claim 2 extra free gifts!

An irresistible offer from Silhouette

Here's a personal invitation from Silhouette to become a regular reader of Desire: and to welcome you we'd like you to have four books, a cuddly teddy bear and a special Mystery Gift - absolutely free and without obligation.

Then, each month you could look forward to receiving 6 more Silhouette Desires delivered direct to your door for just £1.40 each, post and packing free. Plus our newsletter featuring author news, competitions, special offers and lots more.

This invitation comes with no strings attached. You can cancel or suspend your subscription at any time and still keep your free books and gifts.

Its so easy. Send no money now. Simply fill in the coupon below at once and post to: Silhouette Reader Service, FREEPOST, PO Box 236, Croydon, Surrey CR9 9EL.

NO STAMP REQUIRED

YES! Please rush me my 4 Free Silhouette Desires and 2 Free Gifts! Please also reserve me a Reader Service Subscription. If I decide to subscribe I can look forward to receiving 6 brand new Silhouette Desires each month for just £8.40, delivered direct to my door. If I choose not to subscribe I shall write to you within 10 days - but I am free to keep the books and gifts. I can cancel or suspend my subscription at any time. I am over 18. Please write in BLOCK CAPITALS.

Mrs/Miss/Ms/Mr

EP01S

Address

Postcode
(Please don't forget to include your postcode)

Signature